Issue 13
February - March 2019

Lezli Robyn & Tina Smith, Editors
Shahid Mahmud, Publisher

Contents

Published by Arc Manor/Heart's Nest Press
P.O. Box 10339
Rockville, MD 20849-0339

Heart's Kiss is published in February, April, June, August, October and December.

www.HeartsKiss.com

Pleaee refer to our website for information on how to submit material for *Heart's Kiss* magazine.

Available by subscription (www.HeartsKiss.com) or through your favorite online store (Amazon.com, BN.com, etc.).

ISBN: 978-1-61242-448-4

FOREIGN LANGUAGE RIGHTS: Please refer all inquiries pertaining to foreign language rights to Shahid Mahmud, Arc Manor, P.O. Box 10339, Rockville, MD 20849-0339. Tel: 1-240-645-2214. Fax 1-310-388-8440. Email admin@ArcManor.com.

www.HeartsKiss.com

Back Issues

Digital Subscriptions

Paper Subscriptions

...and more

OPENING EDITORIAL

by Tina Smith

Valentine's Day. Homemade cards, surprise flowers, chocolates—as soon as the New Year is rung in the stores fill with reds and pinks and pastel-pressed sugar candies that declare little sweet nothings. Some dread it for its commercialness or a reminder of lost chances. Some embrace it for the chance to connect with those for whom we care the most. Love it or hate it, it's the holiday of romance and that means *Heart's Kiss* wants to celebrate it. And boy, have we this month!

After choosing a holiday theme for our last issue we looked ahead to the next year of the magazine and thought we couldn't pass up another themed issue. So many of our writers took up the challenge. Returning to our magazine, we have fan favorite L. Penelope with a very fun office romance of sorts with the first part of "Before I Break." Luce and Mat will have you rooting for them, from helping a lost child find his parents, to getting trapped together after an earthquake—fate keeps forcing these two resistant romantics together. Our second contemporary offering is a reprint of Jacqueline Seewald's, "Just One Look," where a romance on a cruise ship leads the heroine to go without her glasses to impress the hotty, but he's into the real her, glasses and all. Then we have Alice Faris with a romantic comedy. Can love be manufactured in a laboratory? Two characters venture into an experiment to find out in "Late for Valentine's," but one of them isn't truly a participant in the study.

Paranormal romance is one of my favorite genres and I'm so happy to have two to showcase this issue. The wonderful Petronella Glover returns with "A Wintery Tail," set on the beaches during Australia Day festivities. When the hero has a fishy secret, but the heroine also understands what it's like to be different, sparks fly in this erotic novelette about embracing diversity to find your heart's true desire. And Rei Rosenquist's "A Real Ace V-Day," examines several facets of love, such as the depth of companionship through the lens of a gritty science fiction romance.

If it's historical romance that gets your heart a flutter, then we have a dose of that too. Meghan Ewald is back with a story set in 1836 during the Battle of the Alamo, with "Women Hollering Creek." A laundry woman is in hiding from her abusive husband, but her attraction to a kind soldier brings her hope and new possibilities.

For our non-fiction offerings this issue, we have not one but two interviews with bestselling Australian authors. Popular regency romance writer, Stephanie Laurens, sat down with co-editor Lezli Robyn to talk about her prolific career, how she got her pseudonym and the state of the publishing industry. Lezli Robyn also extended her interview with Juliet Marillier, getting to the heart of what makes her historical fiction tick. With all those Aussies in our table of contents (including my co-editor!), and a story set on Australia day, this co-editor has to wonder if Lezli has been planning a down under takeover for this issue!

What is romance without the tearjerkers too? Julie Pitzel, our columnist, discusses why we love to cry, when those times are needed, why we sometimes choose a happy ending, and what is better suited for our emotional health. "I'll Cry if I Want To" is a fun look into the science of sadness in our literature. And after all that, if you're still looking for more to read, C.S. DeAvilla has a new list of recent releases and some old gems that will keep you entertained through to Easter.

Oh gosh, they haven't started decorating the stores with bunnies and pastels yet, have they? One holiday at a time! I like to spend a little time appreciating them, just as I do a good love story, like the ones we offer you in this issue, dear reader. Lezli and I hope you enjoy.

Once upon a time, #1 New York Times *bestselling author Stephanie Laurens was a research scientist. Fate stepped in, left her with no new Regency-set romances to escape into, so she wrote one…and became a published author, which, she discovered, is a lot more fun. Her novels set in Regency England have captivated readers around the globe, making her one of the romance world's most beloved and popular authors. A* Conquest Impossible to Resist *is her next upcoming novel (March 14, 2019), another instalment in the Cynster Next Generation Novels and her seventy-third published work.*

HEART'S KISS INTERVIEWS STEPHANIE LAURENS

by Lezli Robyn

I had the pleasure of interviewing Stephanie Laurens recently and I am happy to report that she is just as warm and fascinating as her books. I've been wanting to meet her since I picked up the first Cynster book a dozen years ago. It was great to be able to pull back the curtain and find out what it takes to create such breathtaking regency books.

Lezli Robyn: Hello, Stephanie!

Stephanie Laurens: Hello! How are you?

LR: I'm great, now that I'm talking to you. And you?

SL: I'm very well!

LR: Thank you very much for agreeing to do this interview. Not that you knew, but I have been trying to make this interview happen for the past year, since I became co-editor. You're the first romance author I ever read.

SL: Oh, wow. That's wonderful.

LR: And you're an Aussie—you're from my neck of the woods. Gotta represent.

SL: *laughs* Exactly! That's right!

LR: Obviously, the standard first question I ask is, how did you start writing?

SL: I actually ran out of books to read. Well, of the sort that I wanted to read, anyway. I was a senior scientist, so I was spending a lot of time writing grant requests, and also assessing other people's grant requests. Scientific writing is extremely dry, so I would go home and want to read a regency romance—I was into those at the time.

LR: Ah, yes.

SL: In those days, there was only two brought into Australia per month, from Mills & Boon. That was in the eighties.

LR: Wow.

SL: I had read all their previously published books, so there was only two a month I could consume. And that just was not enough, when you are a big reader. So, one day, I was so frustrated that I sat down and started writing. I kept writing after the kids were in bed. I'd just sit down and fire up the computer, and instead of reading a book I started writing a book.

LR: I'm so relieved that the online book buying world didn't exist back then, because otherwise you might never have written. You would have had access to all of the books in the world.

SL: *laughs* Oh, no. That's right!

Eventually, when I finished writing the book, I did not know what to do with it. I thought "It isn't that bad, but what do I do next?" I think it was my mother, in the end, who suggested I send it to Mills & Boon in London, and I did.

They didn't accept it straight away. I had to rejig it a little. Luckily, I did not have to change much. It was more of a balance issue between the adventure side of things and the romance side of things. Once I had done that, they bought it, and that was it—that was how I started my career.

LR: That is amazing.

Where did the kernel of idea come from for doing the Cynster family of books? One thing I love is when I read a novel and discover there is a plot and two romantic leads for the one book, but they're all part of a bigger tapestry and the characters can be seen as secondary characters in other books in the series. How did that come about?

SL: That came about because I was listening to Queen, *We Will Rock You*. It was actually playing on the stereo in the next room. I could both hear it and feel it—because it was turned up quite loud. I think one of my daughters was playing it at the time; she had just discovered our Queen collection. So she was playing it, and I got this vision in my head of this group of English guys, and it just developed from there.

LR: It is amazing how many story ideas are inspired by music. I have to say, I would not think that song would inspire a romance novel, let alone a regency period premise.

SL: Exactly. It wasn't to do with anything specific. I think it was because I was working, I was writing at the time, and the song just connected with that thought.

LR: Did you find it harder to do the research in the start? I assume the first couple of books you were learning it from scratch, so it was more difficult.

SL: No. Actually, I wasn't learning it from scratch. I had always read regency romance—all the Georgette Heyer's, Clare Darcy, a whole heap of others—and we'd lived in England for four years. I was even able to get my hands on a lot of other regency books they used to publish over there that Australians never saw.

I had also done a certain amount of non-fiction research about the regency period, so I really had the background knowledge already. I was writing in a world I was very familiar with at the time.

LR: Fascinating.

SL: What I now look back on, and wonder how the hell I spent so much time doing this, is trying to remember where I had sighted specific houses while in London to use in my books. You had to make places and journeys up in those days because you couldn't just go on Google maps to see…

LR: To see how long it would take one character to ride from one place to another.

SL: Exactly. That's right. There was a lot more guesswork in those times. Nowadays I site things more specifically. It is a very different world. It's more precise and it's a lot faster to find out the information online now.

LR: I noticed that time passes in your novels.

SL: Yes.

LR: Was that a conscious decision you were making from the start, or did you not know the six Cynster books were going to become a continuous series from the beginning? (How many books are there now? Twenty?)

SL: They ended theoretically at twenty and then I started with the next generation series. I knew it was a pretty open-end series, but it's rolled on because the readers still want them, so I keep writing them.

The books are also an—what's the word for it?—an open slather in terms of what interests I can add into them. Whether it's painting and art, or its gardens or horse racing—there are always plenty of green fields to write about.

LR: I have to say, especially regarding the book with the artist as the hero, that the tone you create for your books are distinctly different from title to title. The words you used when the artist was describing his world was language an artist would use. Another hero would have described the scene so differently, but this hero's viewpoint was so beautiful.

SL: Oh, thank you.

LR: Was that a conscious decision? Or was that an instinctive part of creating a character—the fact that as an artist his descriptions of her or the world around him were also so beautifully artistic?

SL: That was a conscious decision. Well, actually, not so much conscious but in that it came about when deliberately shaping the character. I have to know the character really well before I sit down and start to write the story, because the characters have to *drive* the story.

LR: I am one hundred percent with you on that.

SL: I put them into these situations—the situation is usually there from page one, or soon thereafter—and from then on it's working out how the character would respond to that situation, and then how the other character would react, then how they react to each other. There is always a process of progression. I don't devise the story ahead of the characters.

LR: You are not too mechanical about the plot.

SL: No. It's the characters reacting to the situation, foremost, and that reaction shaping the story. It has to be believable for the character to do everything they do, and I develop that as I go along. I can't pre-plan that.

LR: That is very clear to me when I notice the different feel each book provokes with the different lead characters.

I love the Bastion Club series. I noticed the main characters also weave through the Cynster series. Did you have a plan in advance that when a secondary character appears in one of your books that he could end up being the lead character of his own book in the future, or his own series?

SL: To some extent that does happen. For instance, the Barnaby Adair books.

LR: Yes. That series is clearly a next generation Cynster series, yet also promoting non-Cynster secondary characters into lead characters, and it is the beginning of its own series, too.

SL: That's right—exactly. It was always a very organic process, but there are still a couple of characters that I know I have to write stories for but haven't yet. They don't drop off the list—they're still on the list. Don't worry!

LR: *laughs* Oh, good!

SL: It's just a matter of when I can fit them in. There is a character from one of the Bastion Club books,

Lord Justin Vaux. His story's been asked for by readers for so very, very long. So obviously he is going to be written about sometime, but I need time to get to him around all the Cynsters and everyone else.

LR: It's fascinating. When I reread your books, I always spot more character preparation you did in book three, for example, only for it to come to fruition in book ten. And I wonder, how much of it was deliberate, and how much of it was planned.

SL: Yes, sometimes I'm not even aware of how much I unconsciously plan.

LR: So much of writing is organic. Have you found when you've written books that some series are harder to write than others, or specific books?

SL: Well, I have to admit, I'm on book seventy-something now…

LR: Wow.

SL: …and I don't think I've ever had the same experience twice.

LR: That's a good thing though!

SL: *laughs* Yes. There is something different every time. Sometimes a book goes very straightforwardly, but then you come across this and that and you have to pause to deal with an issue. But it's a different issue each time.

I'm not the only one. I know other authors who I'm very close friends with, who have had long, successful careers, that are going through the same issues. No matter how well you organize yourself, in terms of your process, things are always going to be different each book. It just won't be the same twice.

LR: Has your speed changed? Are you a lot quicker now compared to when you started, or does it depend on what book you are writing?

SL: Well, I've become more organized and disciplined. I'm not sure that I'm any faster. In fact, I know I'm not faster or slower than I have ever written. I'm much more steady in my process. Because I do spend a lot of time outlining, if you like. Then I write, and then I edit. I have three specific parts. It's literally about a month and a month and a month. Sometimes it takes more, but I adjust to what the book requires.

The process is more condensed now because my kids are grown and they have kids now. I don't have to spend a lot of time running after children, and picking them up and doing the mom run and all of that.

LR: Yes. You have more writing time and less chasing children time.

SL: Once you get to the point where everything else in your life is taken care of and you can make up your mind to do what you want to do, and then sit down for eight hours or more a day…then you can get a lot more done in a shorter time.

LR: Am I right in believing that your author name is your daughters' names together?

SL: That is correct.

LR: Oh, that is lovely! Do you have two daughters?

SL: Yes.

LR: Oh, that is perfect then—what a lovely legacy for them.

SL: Yes, they know what it means.

LR: It's kind of like you've dedicated every book to them, in a way.

SL: *laughs* Well, yes. I never looked at it that way before.

LR: Their names are on every book—that's great.

SL: Well, my youngest now works with me—in the sense of doing a lot of the business side of things. So that's been useful.

LR: Oh, that is lovely!

Do you have a specific series or a specific book or a sale that you realize was a major milestone in your career?

SL: Well, getting *Devil's Bride* out there, which was—oh, let me count—my tenth book. They always say your tenth book is the one that will take off, and that one certainly did. But as I said, every book is different, so it's really, really hard to pick one out that was more pivotal.

I suppose the other one would be book eighteen of the Cynster series—*The Capture of the Earl of Glencrae*. I deliberately sat down and worked out the three-book arc for that.

LR: That is a beautiful arc, by the way.

SL: Yes. Pulling that off *laughs* was quite a feat.

LR: I love that your books have an overall family arc, and an overall sense of community, with characters from older books appearing in newer books. But it also goes back to your ability to create a specific tone for a book—this trilogy had a specific feel.

I have to say that I loved that one of the lead characters was a scholar, who didn't quite know how to do the big hero moments. It was delightful.

SL: *laughs*

LR: And was it Eliza? Did she say: "No, you can't rescue me. I've got to find out what's happening."

SL: Yes! That was the second one. Yes, indeed.

LR: I love that you can use hero and heroine tropes and turn them on their head.

SL: Yes, that is something I take pleasure in.

LR: Am I right in guessing you complete about three books a year? I assume you take some time off.

SL: Yes, that is about right. Occasionally I have done four, because they are shorter—and part of a series. But, generally it is three releases a year.

Last year, I had, I think—wait, how many was it last year?—I had five releases. But they weren't all long. Only one was a full-length novel. The others were slightly shorter: the Lady Osbaldestone Christmas book and the Casebook of Barnaby Adair ones.

LR: I know they're all your babies, but do you have a favorite hero or heroine out of all of your books?

SL: Not really. Actually, I would have to say no. I'm always most interested in the ones I'm writing next. I think that is Nora's answer, but it is true. The ones that are in your head at any time are the ones you are writing about now.

LR: And I assume they are the ones you are most invested in because you are currently shaping their lives.

SL: Yes, that is exactly it.

LR: I was reading your books in Australia, but buying your books from the United States so I could get the hardcovers. Do you find there is any difference in your fans from different countries?

SL: They are very much the same. I don't think you can put your finger on anything except some of the British—the UK fans—seem to be more aware of the history behind The Black Cobra Quartet, for example. Also, regarding the Bastion Club. They're more aware of the reality of the battles these noblemen went through. So, you do get more—I won't say it is more positive feedback, but it's more knowledgeable feedback, or more appreciation of your efforts.

LR: Yes, I have to say, if I had not looked at the bio on the back page, I would have assumed you were English, with the amount of accurate details you put into your books.

SL: *laughs* Yes, I know. A lot of people don't even know I'm not American.

LR: Exactly, because you have major publishers over there.

SL: I suppose it's because I was always fascinated with that era. I mean, this goes back to my teens. I had been reading about that era—history books and novels—for more than twenty years before I started writing. And as I said, I lived there for four years. I saw things as they really were, so to speak. *laughs*

LR: In our family we have nobility and famous theater actors and actresses. One of them was a friend of Queen Victoria; she used to play in theaters that appear in novels I have read. Since becoming an author I've wanted to write a novel set in that period, with my actual relatives as secondary characters in the background. Maybe the lead characters will go to the theater and see Julia Glover perform.

SL: Yes. *laughs* That would be great.

LR: As a writer the ideas do not turn off. Do you find that you sit down at a specific time to think up new novel plots, or you are making a cup of tea and you suddenly get a brilliant idea?

SL: I usually have the idea for a book just organically—but it's a long time before I can actually write the book. I rarely sit down to write a book when I haven't had more than a year of the story knocking around in the back of my head. By the time I sit down to work on these characters, or on outlining the plot, I've actually got a lot of background worked out in my head already. It makes life a lot easier.

LR: Have you found the industry has changed a lot, since you started?

SL: Immensely. I mean it changed a lot even in the first six years—but once it hit the year 2000 it changed dramatically. I mean, I don't even write with publishers anymore, because it's just not worth my while. It used to be that that was the way forward, but you really have to balance things out nowadays and work out what you are doing.

It is very, very different. An author starting off now would be facing a completely different world and set of decisions, and how she made those decisions would be very different.

LR: Do you think the introduction of ebooks dramatically changed any part of your career? Even in sales?

SL: It wasn't actually the ebooks that caused the biggest change. It certainly was a change, but not a major change. From the viewpoint of an author who was already a *New York Times* bestseller, who was already entrenched in the traditional publishing market—it was Borders going under and the fact that publishers didn't replace Borders with anything that was the problem. They let Borders go under, because they could have saved them, but didn't. They lost all the mass market sales, which was the primary market for romance. And now they are down to about ten percent of what they used to be. That is a huge change.

And what happened is places like Walmart and Target and so on, feared ebooks. They thought ebooks would take up more of their market, so they started cutting back on their shelf space, which *ensured* they lost their market. It was just an implosion.

And now, more and more authors are not dealing with publishers, because they cannot sell much in the way of print books. They physically can't get them in front of readers now.

LR: Is it lack of promotion, too?

SL: No, it is not promotion. It's literally the books not turning up in front of their readers to be seen and bought.

LR: From a reader point of view, you seem to be just as successful, if not more successful, than you have always been. I'm seeing lots of books coming out, lovely covers—I snap them up. Have you found the distribution issue with the print books has been balanced out by the addition of ebook revenue?

SL: Yes—that is correct. What happens is, if you are self-publishing ebooks you're getting seventy percent of the cost as royalties. Whereas if you are publishing ebooks with a publisher, you end up with about fifteen percent of the cost, once the agent takes their cut out your twenty-five percent cut out of the publisher's seventy percent cut. That means you are getting fifteen percent [publishing traditionally] versus seventy percent [self-publishing].

So every self-published ebook sale you make covers a lot of print books. Print books, for an author, are a very low margin book. For an author going through a publisher, you're getting eight percent or ten percent. Even if you are a bestseller you would be getting twelve percent, which is probably the top for a mass market. That is a really small amount of money for a book. So if you are selling ebooks and all the money is going to you, rather than a publisher and

an agent, then, low and behold, you are in a much healthier position.

LR: So basically you are saying the lack of distribution, the increase in ebooks, and the fact you can put ebooks out yourself for more money, makes self-publishing more promising?

SL: Oh, not just more promising—more profitable by a significant margin. A lot of authors don't sit down and do the math. I was blessed because I was a scientist first. *laughs* I can do math.

It is really, really important to find a balance. My last book with Harlequin is going out later this year, and it has been a calculated decision that I still get decent advances from them for the amount of books they can actually sell. But it's the balance between the number you can sell as a self-publisher and the number they can sell, which is not all that different when you take away their ability to sell print books. When there is very little print, you can do the ebooks and audiobooks yourself.

LR: And you get more of a cut, self-publishing.

SL: Yes. By the way, I still do print books—which is about ten to fifteen percent of my sales. They are much higher cost, because they are print-on-demand, but there are enough readers who want to buy them to justify their creation.

LR: I have one last question, and I get some fascinating answers. If you had to pick one male lead from one of your books, and a female lead from another one of your books, to pair together, who would they be?

SL: That's really hard, because you know what I said about the characters driving the whole novel?

LR: Yes.

SL: One of my other issues about characters, for me, is that every female character needs to be the perfect match for the male character, and vice versa. So to split any of them up would be admitting something wasn't right!

LR: *laughs*

SL: That I had somehow failed! *laughs*

LR: That you didn't put the perfect match together.

SL: Exactly!

LR: But see, that is an answer in itself.

SL: Ha!

LR: I do love the answers I get to this question.

SL: I can see a few situations that would be interesting. *laughs* For example, if they were stuck together in a snowstorm in a small place and they couldn't get away from each other—the focus would be on the clash of characters.

LR: I have had one other author say they think a lot of her characters could "get it on" for a weekend, but not necessarily form a happily-ever-after attachment.

SL: *laughs* I can see a lot of interesting moments, that's for sure!

LR: It was lovely to meet you, because as I said, you were the first romance author I ever read. It's not every day you get to meet the author that made you fall in love with the romance field.

SL: Ohhh, thank you. That's a box you can tick off! It's been my pleasure!

LR: Ticking it off now. The pleasure was all mine.

Copyright © 2019 by Lezli Robyn.

Petronella Glover is a multi-genre author whose work has been translated into a dozen languages, including the Catalonian Romance language, where she has won two awards for Best Translated Story. A little quirky, very geeky, and unabashedly romantic, she hopes to one day visit the City of Love, find a bustling café where she can sample their hot chocolate and write her first New York Times *bestseller. This is her sixth appearance in the magazine, and you can find out more about her at www.petronellaglover.com.*

A WINTERY TAIL

by Petronella Glover

I throw the volleyball over to Roger, my roommate, so he can make what is hopefully the final serve, and he lobs it over the net, winning with one powerful thrust of a carpenter-toughened arm. I cheer, leaping playfully onto his back as our opponents pick themselves up off the sand and walk around the net to shake our hands in defeat.

When we've finished with the congratulations and commiserations, I pick up my bag from the side of the court and turn to see what happened with the ball. It's one of mine, so I want to put it back with my gear.

I find it in the arms of one of the most fascinating men I have ever laid eyes on. Tall, dark, and definitely handsome, I walk over to him.

"I believe this is yours," he says, his lovely gold-flecked brown eyes fixing intently on me.

I reach for the ball as he takes me in, obviously noting I'm clothed from head to foot on what must be one of the hottest days of this summer. I throw the ball into the bag, pulling out a water bottle and chugging its entire contents, chucking the empty plastic in the bag before turning my attention back to…who was this guy?

"My name is Iluka." He reaches out a hand to shake mine, and I accept it, feeling a tingle race up my arm upon contact.

His startled look gives me the impression he felt it, too. I mentally shrug. All this exercise must have built up an electrical charge in my body, discharging when we came into contact.

It surely cannot be because this tall drink of a man looks like God's gift to women.

He smiles when I retrieve my hand and watches me as I start tugging awkwardly at my clothes to stop them sticking so much to my body due to sweat. He raises his eyebrows, clearly curious—also looking a little worried.

I pull my hat and sunglasses off, showing him my red-irised peepers and pure white hair. "Winter—nice to meet you."

"Ah…that explains it," he says, gently, relaxing. "Albino?"

I nod, taking in his dark skin, and golden-red tinged black curls. Usually that question irritates me, but I can tell he is expressing concern about me in this sweltering weather, rather than wanting to pry into my genetic make-up. He must realize now I can burn too easily in the heat of the day.

I put the glasses and hat in the bag, take my hair out of its bun, unwrapping it while he watches. "Which side were you rooting for?" I ask him, instantly regretting the correlation my mind makes between "rooting" and this man.

Down, lady. Down. What's wrong with me? It must be heatstroke.

His head tilts to the side, the corners of his mouth turning up again as if in amusement. I realize I must look quite the sight.

"I wasn't rooting for either side," he tells me, eventually. He gestures toward my other roommate, Ruthie, who was sitting along the sidelines. "We're friends, and she mentioned there was a pre-Australia Day gathering down at the beach"—he shrugs—"so I thought I would join in."

His skin is so smooth it looks sculpted, and so dark it's as if he absorbs the sunlight. I detect an accent but can't quite place it. My turn to be rude. "Aboriginal? Torres Strait Islander?"

He snorts. "*Off* Lander would be more accurate."

For a second I wonder if I insulted him, but his grin settles my mind. He does look like he could have come from the Torres Strait Islands, just outside of Queensland proper. But he also has the look of Maori to him, from New Zealand. It is a puzzle, to be sure.

I rummage through my bag for a second bottle, this time only drinking half.

"I haven't seen you here before," I tell him.

He looks at me for a long moment before answering. "I do a lot of traveling. I come and go with the tide."

Ah, probably a surfer. I should have guessed. Lots of beaches, lots of tropical destinations…and, presumably, lots of women.

I'm not sure what to say to him and an awkward silence falls between us. He takes a step forward—

"Iluka! So happy to see you here!"

I pivot to see Ruthie running over, pulling him into an all-too-close hug. I might think she has designs on him, but I know for a fact she is gay—and incredibly affectionate with all those she holds dear.

Which means this guy must all right, to have my roomie's stamp of approval.

Ruthie lets him go and grabs my hand, squeezing it warmly, turning to look at me. "Unfortunately, I have to go now—my shift starts in a halfa. But you were bloody amazing, as usual." Then she focuses back on Iluka. "And you—stop being such a stranger. Sorry we didn't have time to catch up today."

"He can come tomorrow." The words are out of my mouth before I can sensor them.

Ruthie beams. "Oh, that's right! Are you free tomorrow?"

Iluka looks at me, and I feel compelled to explain. "We're having friends over for an early dinner." *And then we're going to the beach after sundown, so I can wear a bikini without the fear of turning into a lobster.*

Something in his gaze shifts, grows warmer, and I feel the urge to fan myself.

What is it about this guy that flusters me so much? I mean, it's not like this is the first time I have seen a handsome man on the beach!

"I'm hot," I tell him, then blush. "Ah, I don't mean it *that* way. I mean, it's time for me to hop into the water to cool off." *In more ways than one.* I look toward the ocean. "It's my reward for playing a game well."

"It was a pleasure to meet you," he tells me, and I can't help but imagine there is more undertone to that line than usual.

I glance back at him, smiling. "Ditto." I put the lid back on the bottle, grimacing at the stale taste of the water—it has soured in the heat—and throw it back into my bag.

I kiss Ruthie on the cheek goodbye, dump my bag with Roger's stuff and break into a short run until the water is hitting my legs and I'm diving straight into the waves. Within seconds I'm emmersed and my tired muscles are sighing at the cool balm of the water.

Exhausted from the game but invigorated by the ocean—or the talk with Iluka. Who am I kidding?—I lift myself up to stand in the waist-deep water and look toward the beach to see he's still watching me, his gaze intent. Distracted, I don't feel the warning tug of a rip forming underneath me. I'm yanked under and into a tunnel of water being sucked out, being pummeled along the bottom of the sea bed as I'm dragged deeper into the ocean.

It's a full minute before the rip spits me out again, and I curse myself for an idiot as I break the surface, shaking my limbs to test for any breaks before treading water. Thank goodness I am wearing clothes, or my skin would have been chafed raw by the sand. I should have checked the water before I dived in. I was just too bloody distracted.

I turn toward the beach and see I'm well beyond the outer crest of the waves. My only hope is to swim across the current, and make my way in slowly, stopping to wave every time I see a surfer coming out to catch the next wave, so they can alert the lifeguard.

Suddenly there are arms around my waist, and I spin within them to see Iluka in the water, pulling me up against his chest so I'm more out of the water. Just the sight of him comforts me and like that stupid damsel in that Hallmark movie with blueberry in its name, I kiss him. Not just a thank you kiss, but a full on I'm-drowning-in-your-eyes kiss.

He doesn't move, stunned. Then he *is* moving, his arms tightening around me, his tongue skating across my lips, asking me for permission to let him in. I do and I'm lost in an undertow of sensations.

Eventually the kiss ends and I open my eyes to see he is as startled as I am.

"I should consider a career as a lifeguard, if this is the thanks I get."

I blush, pushing back from him, and he chuckles, pulling me closer.

"You have to save me first, to claim that title," I tell him. "We're still in the middle of the ocean!" Then I feel it, undulating against my legs.

What—is that scales?

I gasp, pulling back to see a flash of a tail. I really must be hallucinating now.

Shock registers on his face as he looks down at himself. "I'm sorry," he stammers. "I lost control."

Reality comes crashing down. What am I doing? I should not be kissing this man—I only just met him.

I push away from him. "No, I-I'm sorry," I stutter. "I should not have done that."

"Are you okay?" he asks, concern clearly written on his face, but I don't reply.

I see another iridescent flash of scales and look down to confirm the tail is attached to Iluka and not some random fish. The fish *is* Iluka. "You're a-a—"

"I'm a merman," he tells me, but my mind cannot comprehend what my eyes are seeing.

He reaches for me, but I pull back. This can't be happening.

"I lost control of my emotions," he tells me, quietly. "Which meant it broke my focus to keep human form—legs. I know I must look…wrong to you."

I blink, his words breaking through my shock. I know what being different feels like. "No, of course not. You are…breathtaking." And I realize, despite it all, I really do believe that.

With one flex of his tail, Iluka floats forward.

I raise my hand to halt him. "But you are also overwhelming. I need space to think, process."

I suddenly push away and swim for the shore. I can feel him still behind me, shadowing me until I make it to the beach, making sure I am safe, but I don't turn. I don't talk to him. I just run—or rather, swim—away.

What else can I do? Say? If he really is a merman, then we really are oceans apart. How can we ever find common ground?

Our being different is our common ground, I answer myself.

And that kiss, comes the whisper of thought, and it's as if I hear his voice speaking the words. *That kiss is our common ground.*

I yawn, twisting my snowy mane into a bun at the back of my head and open the bedroom door, trying to forget my dreams of kissing mermen. Or rather, one merman in particular. Yum.

I shake my head. I must be going insane. There is no such thing as mermaids. Or mermen. Merfolk? Whatever.

I had to have imagined the tail. It must have been sunstroke. Or maybe my drink had been roofied?

Either way I will have to ask Ruthie if she has Iluka's number so I can apologize for….

For what? Kissing him senseless. He seemed to enjoy that part.

No, I reminded myself. *For fleeing*. I must have come across to him as if I had more than a few screws loose, bolting like that.

I really should text him; apologize.

I make my way down the hall to join in on breakfast—or is it brunch?—with my roommates, when the smell of coffee beans being finely ground assaults my senses, and I opt to hop straight into the bathroom instead, turning on the shower immediately.

I hate the smell of coffee being prepared, and Roger grinds a fresh batch every few days. Nausea swims to the surface whenever I come across a strong scent. Better to shower first, with the knowledge that the smells of breakfast will have lessened by the time I hop out.

It's already getting hot—today's gonna be a scorcher—so I don't turn on the hot tap, using the fresh crispness of the cold water to help wake me. Within minutes I am rubbing shower gel all over my body and thinking about the day ahead.

Australia Day has been one of my favorite holidays since I was little and understood what it meant. Unofficially it's the day we get together and barbeque everything—steaks, snags, caramelized onions, you name it. But unlike Christmas Day we're not roasting five different slabs of meat in the Weber. For some weird reason even Aussies don't understand, we always roast a chicken (or two), a turkey, beef (or sometimes corn beef), pork *with* crackling, and (my personal favorite) lamb for Christmas lunch. On one of the hottest holidays of the year. We must be insane.

But Australia Day, it's a day full of being appreciative for the wonderful country we live in, learning to be more respectful of the people who owned the land before us, and a time to consume charcoaled food and Eskies filled with cold drinks, before going down to the beach to watch all the fireworks going off around Port Phillip Bay.

I turn off the water to hear *Waltzing Matilda* belting down the hallway.

The turning on of music—usually at full pelt if Ruthie has put it on—has always been a hint to her roommates that company will be here soon, and we better get our butts moving. I have always loved the song by Banjo Paterson, often agreeing with the consensus that it would be a better national anthem, but I can't help but make a weird correlation between the events in the song and what happened last night. In my mind, I'm the one going down to the waterhole, instead of a mindless sheep seeking to quench his thirst at the billabong. And instead of a swagman grabbing me with glee, it is a merman....

I shake my head. *Get a grip, Winter. You've got a hinge loose. You only imagined the tail.*

I towel myself off, hearing the door chime. Guests already? I look at the clock—blimey, already midday!—and I realize I have neglected to bring fresh clothes to the bathroom. Bugger.

Untwisting my hair from its bun, I drag a brush through my long white tresses, untangling it as I try to make out the muffled voices down the hall—Roger greeting somebody at the door. I moisturize my face and glance at myself in the fogged-up bathroom mirror, shrugging. Not bad, I suppose. At least my skin has always been flawless, even if colorless. Everything about me is lily white, so putting any kind of foundation or eye products on just makes me look like a clown. I tend not to wear any make-up.

Noticing the music has been turned down to "entertaining guests" level and that Roger is no longer talking to anyone, I wrap myself in my large bath towel and open the door to peek out of the bathroom, making sure that no one is standing in the line of sight of the hallway.

Empty.

I dash out of the bathroom, across the hall and into my room, immediately spinning around to swing the door closed behind me.

"Well now, that is a wonderful sight."

I gasp, turning around to see the man of my dreams, literally, sitting on the edge of my bed. Iluka. Roger must have just let him in!

He stands up, stretching his legs—I knew he had legs!—and makes his way over to me.

All I can do is approximate a fish caught out of water, my mouth open and closing, too stunned to breathe.

What is he doing here? *How* is he here?

"Remember, you invited me," he says, his voice as cajoling as it was yesterday, and I wonder if I spoke out loud. "No," he reassures, "you didn't. It's an ability of my species. To hear thoughts and respond in kind. It's how we talk under water." He registers my shocked response, adding gently. "Did you think we use sign language?"

I don't know what I think. All I know is mermen aren't real. Can't be real.

The corners of his too-kissable lips turn up, wryly, and he stalks his way over me. I instinctively step back, my butt hitting the closed door.

Smiling, he lifts a strand of my hair—"So beautiful"—and runs his hand through it, sending all my emotions into a tail spin.

I look up at him, remembering he's as impressive on land as he is in water. He had to be nearing seven feet, at least! "Why are you here?" I ask again, even though I now remember I kind of invited him, that he is a friend of Ruthie's. He would have asked her for the address.

"I had to see you." *Needed to see you*, I hear him say in my mind.

My eyes widen and I'm at a loss for words. Or maybe I'm not, if he can hear all the tumble of thoughts running through my mind.

He chuckles—suspicion confirmed—and slides his other hand around my towel-covered waist, pulling himself closer to me, anchoring me to him. "I haven't been able to stop thinking about you, my little siren."

I think about the dreams I had last night. "Me neither." Except in them he still had a tail. A swirl of uncertainty deepens in my stomach. Did I really *not* imagine it?

He hesitates, as if finally recognizing my internal struggle with this new reality, and rests his forehead against mine, gently. "We can choose to walk on land, if we wish. We just never usually wish it." His arms tighten around me, sending a thrill down my body. "I had incentive this time." *You.*

He raises his head up to brush his lips over my forehead in a soothing kiss, then each eye. By the time his delicious mouth reaches mine I'm already short of breath. Then his lips descend, and I am lost in a swell of feeling.

I raise my hands up over his taunt chest to grip onto his shoulders, like I'm clutching at a buoy to hold myself above water, and he deepens the kiss, his tongue running along the seam of my mouth until I open it.

He surges in and again it's like we're in the ocean. The floor disappears from beneath my feet as I get swept up by the feel of his tongue swirling in my mouth, the kiss deepening until he lifts me off the ground so I can wrap my legs around his waist.

He nips my bottom lip and I groan. This guy is too good to be true. A literal wet dream.

He pulls back from me, his dark brown eyes meeting my red ones. "I am real. This is real." *We are real.*

"You always seem to say the most important words with your mind," I point out, fascinated.

He chuckles again. "You are observant. My inclination is to talk to you that way all the time, but I know this is all new to you. Believe it or not, considering the moment we just had, I don't actually want to overwhelm you, or scare you off, like yesterday."

I hear the note of uncertainty in his voice as he speaks those last words and realize this must be new to him too. Falling in love with a…what am I?

A land girl.

I must pale—literally—in comparison to the women of his race, with their beautiful tails. I must—

You are perfect, just the way you are, he interrupts with a firmness that confirms that protective streak I had noticed in the water. The one that tried to comfort me in all that strangeness.

With one of his arms secured under my backside, holding me to him, he moves his other hand to the curve of my breast, tracing one taunt nipple, which instantly responds to his attention.

I gasp, not only from the pleasure, but from the realization that I'm now naked. Sometime during our interlude I became completely starkers, the towel having slid off in protest of his passionate ministrations.

You're safe with me, he says simply, and I'm inclined to believe him, but I blush all the same.

When I think about it, this entire relationship can only happen *if* I believe in his existence.

He smiles, and his pleasure lightens up the room, coalescing into a deep warmth between my legs. *I want you*, I tell him shyly, trying this whole thought-telepathy thing out.

The passion in his gaze, the strength I feel radiating out of his body, intensifies. His mouth claims mine again and we're soon lost in a maelstrom of feeling, hearts and bodies molding to each other, becoming indistinguishable from each other.

Eventually, he pauses for air—"I thought merfolk don't need oxygen?" I say, prompting a laugh—and he lessens his grip on me, slowly rocking back and forth into my hips, sensually. Showing me the promise of more.

I groan. "We have to stop," I tell him, reluctantly. "Roommates. Brunch. Not enough privacy."

He nods, his loose black curls almost iridescent in the light filtering through my window. "Are we going to the beach later?" he asks quietly, with intensity, and I swear the room gets warmer.

Definitely. *Most definitely.* "My roommates and I are planning on watching the fireworks on the Mornington Peninsula tonight. Do you want to join us?"

"Yes." He carefully puts me down and I get dressed, surprised to no longer be nervous around him. All I feel is anticipation.

He studies me, now covered in a dress and belt, both pastel in shade, so less harsh in contrast to my skin tone. "I can see the appeal of clothes now. They definitely…highlight aspects of your beauty." *But I think you will be most beautiful when you are naked beneath me….*

I don't think I can get any hotter, but then the implications of those words rush through my body to pool in my center. If I was already in water, I'm sure steam would be coming off me. "Will you be…? I mean, can you…"

He grins, just when I thought he couldn't get any sexier. *Yes, I can be inside you in this form, or when I have my tail.* His head tilts to the side, considering me. *But I think you'll find the latter more, ah, satisfying.*

I blush deeper—the only way any color shows on my skin—and duck my head.

He reaches for my hand, lacing his fingers through mine, squeezing them reassuringly. "Shall we go eat?"

I smile, tummy rumbling, suddenly unable to think of anything I want more. Well, maybe what he just intimated, but otherwise….

Again, that lovely laughter of his peals through the room as he opens the door. *Soon, my siren. Soon.*

The air is heavy with the leftover heat of the day, the evening breeze coming off the ocean a cool balm, helping us relax after a sweltering afternoon. When I bolted off the beach yesterday, I had no idea

I would have a date when I returned the next day. But now I'm reclining in the sand, leaning my back against Iluka's warm chest, his arm lying protectively around my waist as I sit encircled between his legs.

I look down at them, his strong thighs and tautly-muscled shins, and wonder. While his legs look normal—impressively toned, even—I have to admit I can't stop thinking that he usually has (wears?) a tail. That he *should* have a tail. Now that my fear of the unknown has worn off, I want to see it, touch it. Assure myself this is not a dream. That *he* is not a dream.

I hear a chuckle in my mind and Iluka nuzzles the back of my neck, kissing me. *You will see it soon. When everyone leaves.*

A shiver of excitement runs down my spine and I realize I need to distract myself. Australia Day celebrations are being packed up all over the beach, now the fireworks are over, but my friends are still here. I can't keep on behaving like I'm in heat or something.

Again, I hear his laughter and feel my cheeks burning up. This whole telepathy thing is a lot to get used to.

I reach toward the Esky, rummaging through the ice to grab out a Lift—I need the quench of a tangy lemon soda to cool me down. I fumble, almost dropping it, until I feel Iluka's hand wrap around mine, steadying me.

"You seem so distracted tonight, Winny."

I grimace, turning to the owner of the teasing words: Becca, Roger's girlfriend. I put the drink down in the sand, trying to think up an excuse. "It's the fireworks. The loud sounds have jangled my nerves."

Becca stands up, gesturing to Roger to follow suit. "The fireworks finished fifteen minutes ago. Surely they can't *still* be affecting you."

The fireworks had been both spectacular and loud. Maybe not as impressive as the display on New Year's Eve—the major towns go all out, especially around the bay—but the brilliant bursts of color and light had almost been as distracting as Iluka. Almost.

Roger throws me an apologetic expression and turns to Ruthie, who is chatting to her twin, nicknamed Red for her ginger hair. "Ready to pack it in?"

Ruthie frowns, glancing over at her sister, then Roger. "It's not like you to call it a night so early."

Red is a little quicker on the uptake. "Ah…he probably has work tomorrow, as do I. Want me to give you a lift, twinling?"

Ruthie suddenly looks at me and then Iluka, and beams. "Ah, yes. That'll be grand."

They help each other up, shaking off their towels and packing up their Esky. I ask Roger to take everything but my keys and a towel, because I suspect I won't be staying on the sand too much longer and don't want to leave my things unattended.

I can feel Iluka's pleasure at my observation—how is that possible?—and I hear his voice in my mind like a caress, a promise. *Into the water, baby.* He disentangles himself from me gracefully, reluctantly, and stands up. *I'll join you soon.* He walks away from me to help Becca and Roger carry the last of their stuff to the car, leaving me to wonder what that gorgeous toosh of his will look like covered in scales.

I stand up and turn back to the ocean, mesmerized by the sight of the Milky Way snaking across the sky until it dips into the gentle expanse of water. I can't help but wonder if Iluka's people also have Dreamtime Stories about how the stars came to be, like the Aborigines. I remember his cryptic reply when I had originally wondered if he was of Torres Strait Islander extraction and he had said, "*Off* Lander would be more accurate."

Now I know why he said that, but I also wonder how closely he's related to the Australian people.

We share bloodlines with many indigenous Islander people—not exclusively those of Australia. It's why so many think I look Maori when in New Zealand, or Polynesian when in Tahiti.

Does that mean you're considered part of the human species?

In truth, we are not the same people, but we are—his words deepen quite suggestively—*very compatible.* I hear Iluka saying goodbye to my friends as their cars pull out onto the main road, then his feet crunching in the sand as he walks back to me. *Generations of finding Mates among the races who walk the land have provided us with a certain camouflage.*

"No matter where you wash up, you look like you belong—well, as soon as you ditch your tail, that is."

"Exactly." His arms slide around my waist from behind, pulling me back against his chest. "My name means 'by the sea' in Bunjalang—an

Aboriginal language. It is a town name in New South Wales, too, where it is said my father used to walk the land."

I look down at his arms, so dark against my skin—so full of history, tenderness. "I look forward to finding out more about your people."

He pulls away from me and I spin around, at first wondering if I said anything wrong. Maybe he can't talk about his people—some kind of secrecy pledge. Then I realize he is pulling his shirt off, throwing it onto the beach beside my towel and keys.

The moonlight glides over his skin, the shadows defining how broad his shoulders are, how big the muscles—he's built like an Olympic swimmer. I watch him unbutton his board shorts and realize that while *I* might not be anxious at the thought of being naked in front of him again, given how amazing he made me feel in my bedroom, the thought of seeing *him* fully naked floods me with nervousness.

With his hands still on the partially-open zip, he looks up at me. "I'm so used to nakedness—I wasn't thinking. The scales usually cover me more than these shorts do."

I start to tell him, "I don't mind, I just wasn't expecting it," but he leaves his board shorts on and reaches for me, picking me up, kissing me soundly. I wrap my legs around his waist, losing myself in the moment.

We'll go slow, he tells me as he finishes up the kiss, then walks into the water.

"Wait!" I exclaim, putting both hands on his chest as if to halt him.

He stops immediately; I can feel his heart thudding against my palm. I quickly glance down the beach, checking that everyone had indeed gone, then reach behind my back to undo the string on my bikini top. Within seconds it is off and flying into the pile of clothes on the beach.

Iluka's breath quickens and his grip tightens, but he doesn't move his eyes from mine. "May I?" he asks.

I feel one of his hands move to tug on one of the ties at the side of my bikini bottoms, and I nod.

That is all the permission he needs. He undoes one knot, then shifts me in his arms so he can undo the tie on the other side, grabbing the material and yanking it off me, exposing me completely to the elements. To him.

I gasp, because suddenly I'm in the water, too, and it's bloody freezing.

I clench my legs tighter around his waist and he groans, spearing one hand through my hair as his mouth plunders mine.

I'm once again lost in a maelstrom of emotions as he takes us deeper into the ocean, the feeling of salt water against my nakedness as overwhelming as his attentions on me. Within moments I'm tingling with arousal, warming up despite the chill of the water.

Iluka eventually halts the kiss, pulling back a little to look down between us, studying my body with a fierce passion in his eyes. "So beautiful."

His voice is reverent, like I'm something to be treasured instead of that weird geeky girl with freakish genes.

"You are perfect," he tells me, correcting me. "Made of moonlight."

His words touch me, deeper than where my heart resides. They touch my soul.

I lean forward again and kiss him slowly, sensually—a kiss full of heart. His lips open and I suck on his bottom one, coaxing another groan out of him.

One of his hands slides down over the curve of my backside, kneading it rhythmically at first, then more urgently, and I gasp.

Lifting me higher with seemingly no effort, he latches his mouth onto one of my nipples and starts laving it with his tongue, nipping it, then sucking it fiercely as I wrap my arms around his neck, my fingers digging into his back as I throw my head back in pleasure.

No matter how hard I mewl he doesn't let up, except to switch to the other breast, until I'm wet in more ways than one and sliding down his body again to instinctively rock my hips against his erection.

I need you, he says. *I can feel your heat and it is driving me crazy.*

I still, opening my eyes to look at him. How do I say it?

He waits, and when I don't answer says, *I won't judge.*

I hesitate, self-conscious this had not come up earlier…before…. *I've never done this before.*

His eyes register surprise when he realizes I don't just mean sex with a merman.

I mean sex, period.

"I was always…the different one," I tell him, using my words, worried I'll overload him with embarrassing emotions if I try to communicate telepathically.

His eyes soften, and he rests his head against mine. *Our people Mate for life.*

He waits for the implications of his words to hit me. They do, with hurricane force. "You have not been with anyone else, either?" I'm shocked. I know he's at least ten years older than me. I've seen women drooling over him. He could have had any woman on this beach tonight; he's irresistible.

He pulls back, shaking his head. *It's not like that.*

"But surely you have mermaids you could have… you know…"

No. Well…I mean, yes, they do exist. But…no. Not for me.

The spark of happiness at knowing he has never been with another woman—tail or no tail—cuts through my surprise. "But how can I be your Mate if I'm not a mermaid? How is that possible?"

He raises a hand to my face, cupping it, stroking his thumb tenderly over my bottom lip. *Love is love. It knows no boundaries.* He starts rocking against me, slowly at first, then faster. *I just know you are mine. Every instinct within me tells me this is so.*

I feel the import of his words, what they mean to him. I need to show him he's not alone in this. *I feel the same way,* I tell him, speaking in the way of his people, putting as much emotion into my words as I can.

He surges forward again, and suddenly we're kissing under the water, my back pressed against the ocean floor. It feels so incredibly intimate, so primal—the water surrounding us. Pushing his board shorts down over his hips to free his arousal, I feel the tremor in his body as he fists his hands in the sand.

When he knows I need air he pushes me up to the surface again, but he doesn't follow, sliding down my body until he's kissing my navel, then sliding even farther down to kiss me where I feel the most need. I cry out, clutching at his curls, anchoring his head between my thighs as he starts stroking his tongue in and out of me. I squirm, looking through the water to see him devour me and I'm unable to handle the pleasure. I don't know what this feels like on dry land, but it's bloody incredible to feel the rush of water as he finds my clit, flicking it with his tongue for long tortuous minutes before sucking on it hard.

I shatter and the orgasm is intense, my legs gripping his head as the ripples of pleasure go on and on.

Eventually they subside and I realize he's been under the water this whole time. He really is a merman, even if he still isn't showing me his tail.

I feel his chuckle inside my head. *We're taking it slow, remember?*

You call this *slow?* I ask him, incredulous, unwrapping my legs.

He slides back up my body—sensuously, teasingly—his head breaking the surface of the water to recapture my mouth. I taste me on his lips and it's so erotic; I just can't get enough of him.

The feeling is mutual.

I smile through the kiss as I float against him. I want to wrap my legs around him again—never let him go—and I realize that is a distinctly human mating instinct. Merfolk can't do that with tails.

You're right. And for me, there's nothing sexier. He grips my hips to help guide me. My legs fall around him, feet hooking together at the small of his back. Immediately, I feel his erection pressing against my warmth, his board shorts having disappeared in the tumult of passion and rushing water.

I pull back to see him close his eyes and take a deep breath—he's still holding back. I start rocking against his arousal, back and forth, increasing my rhythm and speed until his hands are clenching my hips, his desire barely restrained.

My siren, he declares, then pulls me up so he can thrust slowly into me. I feel way too small for his length and girth, but he shows me I can take him, only stopping when he hits some kind of obstruction, the barrier most virgins have.

We're both breathless and wanting more. I feel his pleasure at knowing he's the only man to have been inside me, and also a rush of protectiveness as he holds himself steady, wanting to make sure I'm ready.

Please, I tell him, desperate to feel him deep inside me. *I don't want to go slow anymore.*

Iluka doesn't blink. He surges in, and while there's a pinch of pain, I'm swept away by the intensity of being filled by him. He feels amazing.

Are you sure you're okay? he asks me, flexing his hips to stroke into me again.

I gasp my answer, pulling him farther into me with an instinctive clench of my legs and that is what finally sends him over the abyss.

He slides one hand up my back, and in one quick move wraps my hair around it, possessing my mouth as he thrusts into me, hard and fast, again and again, the pressure building in both of us until there is a ripple—I can't think of another word for it—and suddenly he feels different, more powerful. Impossibly he enlarges inside of me, somehow filling me more completely.

I moan when I realize my feet are now rubbing up against scales as he pummels into me, undulating his tail in a way that increases both of our pleasure.

"Oh god." He had told me last time he'd morphed into his natural form, when he lost control of his emotions and could no longer hold human shape. I gasp, feeling like he's too big for me, but wanting more.

Come for me, my siren, he tells me, and I obey, my orgasm so intense that I'm shuddering around him as he thrusts in one last time, falling apart himself.

It is some time before we float back to full consciousness and I run my hand through his hair, tugging it playfully. *They didn't mention* that *in the fairytales.*

He laughs, full bellied and rich, and gently pulls away from me so that his tail is in direct moonlight, studying my face.

I am in awe. *You are so beautiful*, I tell him. I realize I'm just repeating his words of earlier, but there's no other way to describe his impressive form. Brown-black skin lightens into a rich russet tail, undulating back and forth, the moonlight picking up an iridescent shimmer of the same golden-red highlights I saw in his dark curls during the day. He was breathtaking.

And we couldn't look any more different if we tried.

He reaches for me again and rests his forehead against mine. *I am the yin to your yang.*

I can't help but smile. The yin, the dark swirl in the well-known Chinese symbol, is associated with shadows, and the trough of a wave; the yang, the light swirl, represents brightness, passion and growth. *We are more well-matched than I originally thought.*

I never doubted it. You are my Mate.

The warmth I feel has nothing to do with arousal this time, although I suspect that will be returning shortly. I mean, look at him.

Iluka laughs, then gestures toward the beach. *First we drink*, he tells me, reminding me of my long-abandoned can of Lift. *Then*, he raises one eyebrow suggestively, *I believe I told you you'd look most beautiful lying beneath me….*

I look at the waves lapping the shore, their regular rhythm reminding me of Iluka filling me, surge after surge, and I imagine lying in the shallows, Iluka on top of me, his tail undulating as he thrusts into me, in beat with the waves. In and out. In and out.

A perfect fit.

Soon, my love. Soon.

Copyright © 2019 by Petronella Glover.

Meghan Ewald was born and raised in northern California. She now makes her home in Texas with her husband, their two children, one very happy rescue dog and a spoiled rotten house rabbit. Meghan writes fiction in the wee hours of the morning before going to her full-time job playing with NASA space suits. She loves good coffee, reading, working out and writing. When not writing fiction, Meghan blogs over at http://gettingthewordswrong.com/. She loves to hear from readers. You can reach her at gettingthewordswrong@gmail.com.

WOMAN HOLLERING CREEK

by Meghan Ewald

Maria Perez bent over the dirty clothing soaking in the creek. The strong sun pounded down on her back. She wiped the sweat from the side of her face. The summer of 1836 hadn't quite reached the Misión San Antonio de Valero in Mexico's Tejas territory yet, but it was on its way. Already her brown skin darkened from the renewed strength of the sun.

The cool water of the creek felt good on her bare feet, and she wished she could climb in, but there were too many people watching. She sighed. She was a stranger here in this little community, and though she'd been here for months and had caused no trouble, she knew people talked. People always talked. They questioned cautiously where her husband was, why she was travelling alone, who her people were. No, it would not do to draw more attention to herself. Attention led to rumors and rumors led to her being found by those she'd rather not be found by. Other washer women ranged up and down the creek, their children playing noisily along its banks. Maria straightened from the heavy, water-logged clothing and knuckled her back.

Spring flowers sprayed the banks of the creek vibrant with reds and golds and blues and pinks. Maria hummed a tune her mother had sung while she did laundry when Maria was a child. Her mother would have loved those flowers by the creek. A tear coursed down Maria's cheek and dropped onto a nearby bluebonnet at her feet. The flower shimmered as her tear touched it. Maria drew in a breath and glanced to see if anyone else had noticed. No one was looking at her. Maria dashed the tears away with the back of her hand. Already the flower appeared normal again. Still beautiful but a more ordinary beauty. Maria breathed a sigh of relief then cursed herself a fool. She knew better. She always cried when she sang. Her mother had too.

She remembered holding her mother's skirts the first time she'd seen the colors flare, her mother saying, "Do you see, my Maria? Do you see our song makes the colors more beautiful?" And it had. All about them the spring flowers blazed colors bright as the sun. Maria had looked up then to see her tears coursing down her mother's face too. Maria smiled and her heart ached for her mother. What would her mother make of her now? A runaway wife hiding as a washer woman from the man she'd married.

She ought to finish these clothes. Her customers would not pay if they were still dirty when she returned them.

"That's quite a singing voice you have there."

Maria's breath caught and she spun around. Behind her stood a tall, bearded man with piercing blue eyes. He wore a disheveled Texas Revolutionary uniform, the kind they wore just west of here at the Misión San Antonio de Valero. In his hands he held a bundle of clothing. "I was told I'd find the washer woman down by the creek." He held the bundle out to her, a sheepish look on his face. "Commanding officer said not to come back until it was all presentable. I've never done my own clothes before. My ma always did them." He held the bundle of clothes out to her.

Maria forced her pounding heart to calm. Had he seen? She took the bundle of clothes. "Well, that's all right mister…"

"Kimble. George Kimble."

"Yes, Mr. Kimble. I charge a flat fee of three dollars, and anything that needs special attention I ask five cents an hour."

George Kimble scratched his beard. "That seems a bit steep, Miss…"

"Lopez," Maria lied, defaulting to her maiden name. She thrust the bundle of clothing back at him. "Those are my rates, Mr. Kimble. But you won't find better quality work along the Frio."

"George. Please call me George."

"George, then. It was a pleasure to meet you, but I don't work for free."

George blinked in surprise, and Maria bit the inside of her cheek. She'd been too direct. She'd always been too direct. Martin had backhanded her more than once for it, and yet she could not speak any other way. So she stopped talking and hoped this man would not draw more attention to her. She could already see curious eyes glance at them then quickly turn back to their gossiping.

Then George smiled, crinkling the corner of his eyes. Maria could not help but wonder at how piercingly blue they were. "No, ma'am," he said, his blue eyes twinkling. "Of course you don't." He offered her the bundle again. "Miss Lopez, I would be glad to pay for quality work." Maria nodded and took the proffered bundle of clothing. "In fact, I'll pay you double. If, that is, you'll let me hang about and learn to do it for myself." Her hands froze over his.

Had it been a trap? *Did Martin send him?* She quickly banished her paranoid thoughts. Martin had nothing but contempt for the Revolutionaries. He would not associate with this man. But she didn't know this man. Maria eyed him, really taking him in. He was tall and outweighed her by at least fifty pounds. Would anyone come to help her if the situation turned sour?

"I don't know about that, Mr. Kimble," Maria said. "People talk around here. We'd cause quite a bit of fuss."

"No, I imagine that would not do." His eyes still twinkled with held in laughter. "I'll stay here on the bank and watch. You can instruct me from a distance. Or, perhaps, you'd prefer one of your competitors to get my business?"

Maria sniffed. "You'd learn nothing from them. They do terrible work." Maria eyed him. He seemed innocent enough with his American charm, but Maria didn't trust men, especially the pretty ones. And this one needed a shave. That beard did him no favors. Maria thought of the extra money and the thick stick she had hidden in the bushes. She knew how to use it if she needed. After a moment, she nodded and accepted the bundle.

"Then it's settled." He extended his hand and Maria flinched. She hated herself for it, hated he'd seen it. His eyes softened with something more serious. "Shall we shake on it?"

Maria forced herself to nod and took his hand. His palm was warm and callused against hers. She made herself grip it and firmly shake and was satisfied to see him blink with surprise at her grip. "You have a deal, Mr. Kimble."

Some of the ladies along the bank watched and smiled knowingly. Maria knew they talked and could not understand why a beautiful young woman wasn't married and why she lived alone. But they were all migrants and from somewhere else and so had learned not to ask too many questions.

An hour later his clothes were clean and drying in the sun on the grass beside them. Maria had found him a sharp student and had only had to explain each step one time. While they waited for the clothing to dry, they sat on the bank in comfortable silence, him laid back in the grass, his hat tipped over his eyes shielding them from the afternoon sun. Ever aware of prying eyes and spreading rumors, Maria sat facing him a socially-appropriate distance away with her chin on her knees, her arms wrapped demurely around her skirts. When, she wondered, had she last been comfortable with a man, and could not think of a time.

"That's a lovely song you're humming. Is that the one you were singing when I walked up?"

Maria stiffened, her eyes darting around in alarm. She hadn't been aware she'd been humming. Although the flowers and grass about her appeared brighter. She didn't think he'd seen and his hat blocked any attempt to read his expression.

"Just something my mother taught me. It was a long time ago." She blinked, changing the subject. "Tell me about yourself, Mr. Kimble. How old are you?" Men loved to talk about themselves. Martin certainly had. Lying in bed he'd told her all his grand schemes and plans, talked about his undying hate of the traitorous Revolutionaries. She'd learned if she sounded interested and kept him talking he was less inclined to strike her.

"Turned thirty-three at my last birthday. And there ain't much to tell."

"Just the same. I like to know who my clients are." In truth, she cared little who her clients were as long as they paid on time. But she did not want to talk

about her song. And the grass and flowers were fading back to their normal colors. She didn't want him to see that either.

"Well, I was born in 1803 in Beechwoods, Pennsylvania. My pa's name was Chester, my mother, Lucy."

"Pennsylvania. That's a long way from here."

George nodded and sat up, pushing his cap to show more of his face. Maria noted with relief that the surrounding colors were something more normal.

"We moved around quite a bit. Once to upstate New York and then to St. Clair County in Michigan. In 1825, when I was 22, I moved to the Green DeWitt Colony."

Maria's eyes widened at this.

"You know the name?"

Maria nodded and chose her words carefully. "That was the first battle, wasn't it? Of the Tejas Revolution?"

George nodded. "You do know it."

"I heard someone talking about it." That someone had been Martin, but that was her business and there was no reason to say that name aloud. "Tell me, Mr. Kimble, do you think the fighting will come here?"

"I hope not, but if it does, we'll handle it." Maria had her doubts. She'd seen Martin's army at work. She kept her reservations to herself.

"How about you, Maria?"

Maria watched him warily. "What about me?"

"Well," he said, a mischievous twinkle in his eyes. They were nearly white they were so crystalline blue, Maria thought. "Same questions. How old are you? Or am I not supposed to ask that?"

"I'm twenty-eight, and no you're not supposed to ask that," Maria said primly.

"Twenty-eight and not married?"

Maria went cold. "I don't want to talk about myself, George."

They parted that day as friends, George with a bundle of clean clothing, and Maria with the pleasant tiredness of a good day's work. Maria bid the tall man farewell and wondered if she'd ever see him again.

Foolish woman, she thought, *haven't you had enough of men? Do you want Martin to find you? Because he will if rumors spread too far. Better he stays away.*

But George Kimble did not stay away. He came back the next day and the next, each day carrying some item that needed laundering. And each day she found herself looking for him, anticipating his arrival. She knew this was a mistake, knew she should send him away. But she liked him and maybe more than liked him, though she would not fully acknowledge that feeling yet. No, that was a dangerous feeling better left buried deep and never looked at in the sunlight. The war between happy anticipation and the dread at being found by Martin tied her stomach into a knot that swelled in size each day.

On the third morning George offered her a bouquet of wild flowers. The gesture drew attention from the other woman washing along the bank. They smiled and whispered with winks her way. Then gossip in town about the white man in love with the Mexican washerwoman. Any talk about her was bad. Talk had a way of spreading and if someone were to carry the rumors and her description to Santa Anna's army, Martin would find her. The thought of seeing Martin again made her stomach churn.

At the very least he'd beat her, and probably quite badly. As bad as the time she'd lost the baby. She flashed back to that terrible night she'd told him she was pregnant. She'd been four months along at least and was just barely starting to show. She'd nervously hoped for Martin's excitement. Instead when he'd struck her across the face, knocking away her happy smile.

"Martin, why did you do th—?"

Her question cut off when he punched her in the stomach. Her lungs burned, shocked from the impact, and she fell to the floor. He kicked. And kicked. Her hands curled around her swollen stomach to protect the new life inside her. It hadn't helped. The baby had died, and she'd nearly died with it.

As soon as she'd been able, she'd run away. If she was found, she did not think Martin would let her live to run away again. Or if he did let her live, she'd be a slave, only allowed out to sing her song and shut up again after healing him and his men when they lost a battle.

She saw other people looking at George standing there, proffering the flowers like an idiot child. She snatched the flowers from his hands and flung them away into a bush near the creek. Hurt cramped George's face and she felt a pang of regret. All it did was serve as a microscope as all the women paused

their washing to watch the drama. Maria grabbed George's arm and though she was half his size at least, she dragged him away. There was no helping the rumors that would spring up from being alone with him, but it was better than him standing there with those damned flowers.

When they were a safe distance from prying eyes, she rounded on him. "You cannot bring me flowers, George."

"You don't like flowers? They seem prettier around you. Brighter somehow. What? Did I say something wrong? Maria, all the color just left your face. Here, sit down."

George guided her sit beneath a tree. She sat down heavily, folded her arms across her knees and put her head down. She forced herself to breathe deeply in the small privacy she'd created. Her thoughts raced.

So he had noticed. If George had noticed, others surely would too. She would need to leave. Find a new place. Or Martin would find her and Maria didn't like to think of what that reunion would look like.

"Maria?" Warm hands enfolded hers and she lifted her head. She looked up to meet his gaze and knew with a sinking resignation she was well on her way to being in love with this impossible man before her, so sweet and earnest in his concern. "Maria? Are you all right?"

Jesus Christ and God in Heaven, help me, she prayed.

"You had better sit, George," Maria said. "There's something I need to tell you."

And there on the bank of the creek, where rumors were doubtless flying around down by the water, Maria told what she'd sworn she'd never tell anyone. She told George of marrying Martin and how he'd pursued her, she knew now because he wanted her song, because he'd wanted the healing power passed down from her mother.

"He used me to heal his wounds after every battle."

George frowned. "You mean like a nurse?"

"Not exactly. My song. It heals. That's why the flowers bloom brighter around me. My mother could do it, and I can do it too. That's how he got the legend started. How his men believed he could make them walk away from every battle."

"That's…incredible," George said, sounding both disbelieving and awed. "How did you get away?"

"There's more." Maria swallowed hard. "The how isn't as important as the why." She'd come this far. She might as well tell it all. But she could not look at him while she told it. She looked at her hands, fidgeting and wringing them. Strong, brown hands. Like her mother's.

She could not look at him while she told the story. "He hit me, George. He hurt me. If we weren't married, it would have been called rape, but no one saw it as rape since he was—is—my husband. And when I discovered I was pregnant, he took that from me too."

She told him of how she'd lost the baby. How she'd made it here, rescued by members of this community after nearly dying of thirst in the dry Tejas south. She told it all, and the telling was like an infection inside her had been scooped away. The wound left behind was empty and hurt, but it was a clean hurt that promised to heal with time. Tears rolled down her cheeks as she told her story.

"I know he's looking for me. If word of me spreads, he'll find me. And if he finds me, the best I can hope for is he'll kill me. But I don't think he'll do that. I think he'll keep me prisoner. And I don't want to think what my life will be like then."

George said nothing for a moment. Maria looked up and studied his face for any indication of his reaction. His face was grim, his eyes blazed iridescently with barely-controlled fury.

Maria shrank from him. "I'm sorry. I didn't lie to you because you didn't ask, but it was near to a lie. I should have told you I was married. You deserve better than that."

"Maria," George said, stilling his wringing hands by wrapping them in his own. "I am not angry with you. I am angry that anyone would hurt you. And I won't let him take you. I'll protect you, with my life if necessary."

He'd said it with such conviction, Maria believed him. But hope seemed too cruel an emotion to rely on.

A week passed and every day George came to see her down by the creek. The people of the community talked amongst themselves, but they didn't seem to venture beyond the community borders. They didn't trust outsiders, though Maria seemed to be accepted as one of them, and her tall American was accepted with knowing smiles by proxy. Maybe she was safe. Maybe she could stay here. She wanted to stay. She felt safe and she had not felt safe for a long, long time.

One Saturday morning, she strolled alongside George who carried her bundles from the town's one tiny market. She excitedly pointed at the color and craftiness of the art displayed. The street was busy with people running weekend errands. Husbands carrying baskets for their wives or loading them up into wagons.

Two children, a boy and a girl of about five, ran around their family's old wagon playing hide and seek. The girl ran around the front of the wagon shrieking with laughter, her dark hair flying backward over her shoulders. The boy chased after her with a dogged expression on his face, determined to catch his sister. Their mother, a stout woman in a homespun dress, shouted after them in Spanish to be careful.

George and Maria paused to let them run past. George grinned at Maria and she could almost read his thoughts. Then Maria realized what she was doing and pulled herself up short. Was she really so familiar with George now? She supposed she was.

"George, I—" Maria began, but she didn't get to finish what she was going to say. There was a loud crack. Maria and George both turned to look. The axle of the family's old wagon had split and the back collapsed to the dirt. The mother of the children shrieked and beat at the back of the wagon.

"Ayuadame! ¡Mi hijo! ¡Mi hijo!"

Maria and George rushed around to the back of the wagon. Maria gasped at what they saw. Pinned beneath the weight of the wagon was the small boy. George jumped into the fray with a number of other men and together they heaved the heavy wagon off of the child. But Maria could see that the damage had been done. The boy's small body lay broken, his legs at odd angles and he did not open his eyes. The boy's mother shrieked and she fell to her knees trying to scoop the boy into her arms.

"No, don't move him!" Maria caught the woman by the shoulders and pulled her away. "If you move him it will make it worse." The woman struggled against Maria, blind and insane with grief. Her husband grabbed her and held her. He gave Maria a pleading look.

"You help?" His accent was thick, and Maria could tell his English was limited. He was asking if she could help the boy. The man's gaze darted as if searching for some miracle to appear, and she thought he would have asked the question of anyone who stood in front of him. But he hadn't asked anyone. He'd asked her.

Maria made a split-second decision. She nodded once, quickly, and knelt beside the boy's broken body. He seemed even younger lying in the dirt. She laid a hand on his small chest. He was still breathing. Good.

"Maria," George said, kneeling beside her. He spoke low, for her ears only. "Are you sure you want to do this? There are a lot of people."

"I know. I have to. I'm the only one who can." She met George's eyes. Would she be able to find her way into the song with so many eyes watching? She didn't know, but she had to try. "Just keep them back."

George nodded and Maria thought he was relieved to have been given a job. Maria turned her attention to the boy. Behind her, George was telling the onlookers to step away. Maria let the noise of the crowd fade. The world narrowed to her and the boy. Maria closed her eyes and hummed the first bar of the song her mother had taught her so long ago. The feeling of so many eyes on her, like tiny pin pricks on the back of her neck, fell away. Maria softly sang the first few words of her mother's song. With relief, she found they rang true to her ears. Maria sang the song her mother sang to her. She filtered every fear and dream she'd ever had into the song. Dimly she heard people gasp, but that was far away. Maria only had eyes for the boy. Color returned to the boy's cheeks. Maria continued singing until his eyes fluttered open. He smiled up at her. His two front teeth were missing. Maria was glad to see his gums were pink and clean, so it wasn't from the accident.

"Well, hello there," Maria said, smoothing his hair back from his brow.

"*Mamá hay un ángel.*" His missing front teeth made him lisp lightly.

His mother screamed again and rushed forward as Maria sat back. She gathered the boy into her arms and rocked him, babbling her gratitude to Maria, her scraps of English falling away.

There was a din of excitement around her. Everyone could now see the boy was healed where mo-

ments before he'd been broken and dying. George pulled her to her feet and wrapped his arms around her in a happy embrace. Maria fought tears as she pressed her face into his shirt and breathed in his good smell. Rumors would start from this. There was no getting around it. Maybe she'd get lucky and they wouldn't reach her ex-husband before she could leave. She had to leave now. She knew that. Amid the excitement Maria accepted their thanks, and began to make plans.

Martin Perez wanted to throttle the idiot private standing before him in his large officer's tent. The man was a slovenly mess and Martin couldn't abide a messy unit. This man's shirt was untucked, mud on his boots, his beard untrimmed and patchy. How had he been allowed to look this way for even a moment? He must be one of the new recruits. Since Maria left (ran away, his mind whispered, and he ground his teeth), men had died in battle necessitating replacements. Perhaps if Martin killed this idiot man the others would learn to fall in line and this headache would go away. It had started as the man spoke of this rumor and was now ratcheting up to be a real screamer behind his eyes.

Martin's hands itched to wrap around the man's throat, but if he did that, he might not get all of the story and he wanted to know where his wife had run off to more than he wanted anything. Instead he placed both hands down on the heavy, carved desk he had hauled from place to place and set up by scum like this.

"Tell me again," Martin said. He forced his voice to be calm even though his inside wasn't. "Did you see her?"

"N-no, sir. I heard a rumor, sir."

"And what was the rumor, private?"

"As I said before, sir, it is rumored that a woman brought a boy back from the dead. There was an accident in the town, a wagon accident, and a boy was crushed. He should have died, the gossip goes, but a washer woman sang to him and brought him back to life. They are calling her a miracle worker."

Martin picked up the small hand whip he kept on his desk, stood from the desk and paced slowly about the room as he spoke. He almost casually slapped the whip against his other hand. *Slap, slap,*

slap. Martin noted the private's wince each time the whip struck his palm. Martin liked the whip. It served two purposes. It served as an intimidation tactic that had worked for many years now, and it kept his hands busy so they would not stray and kill this idiot man as they so wanted to.

Martin stopped pacing right in front of the private, though he did not give the private the courtesy of turning to face him so the private was left staring at Martin's left shoulder. Martin was a tall man, and he was well aware of how his looming over someone shorter than himself unmanned them. "And who told you this rumor?" Martin did not turn his head to speak to the private.

"A villager, sir. One of my informants."

"And where is this miracle worker now?" Martin spoke softly, turning his gaze to meet the private's frightened eyes. A bead of sweat slid down the private's forehead to his cheek to beneath the starched collar of his stained uniform. "Not far sir," the soldier said.

Martin allowed himself to lose his temper. "Where is she?!" He struck the man with the hand whip. The private fell to his knees clutching his bleeding face in his hands. Martin hit him again and again.

"Near the Misión San Antonio de Valero." The cowering private covered his head with his arms, peeking up from between them. "It is just a rumor, Señor. How could it not be?"

Martin knew better. This was no mere rumor. He strode back to his desk and set the whip down. "You're dismissed, private. And clean yourself up. I will not tolerate slovenliness in my army."

The private scrambled out of the tent. A slow grin curved his lips.

"Luckily for us, we are going there next and we can see for ourselves this miracle worker."

Maria didn't get far. She opened the door to her little house that evening, a bag in her hand, only to find a line of townspeople winding down the road away from her house. Every one of them had another person with them. Some on makeshift crutches, some with bandages wrapped around their heads. The woman at the front of the line carried an infant wrapped in swaddling with another young girl shyly peeking around her mother's skirts. And she wasn't the only one. A number of women had children with them. The blatant, shining hope in their eyes made Maria's stomach plummet. An expectant hush fell over the crowd when she opened the door.

She spotted George helping an old man with an injured foot. George handed him off to another person in the crowd and walked up to meet her.

"George, I can't—" Maria began before her throat closed with choked back tears.

"You can't leave them," George said gently. "You would never forgive yourself."

"Did you do this?" Maria glared up at him through tears.

"No. They would have come with or without me. But they aren't wrong for coming."

Maria sagged against the doorframe and stared down the line of anxious faces. Her bag slipped from her numb fingers to the floor. "He'll find me, George."

George put a gentle finger under her chin and tipped her brown eyes up to meet his blue. "We will not let him have you," he said. "*I* will not." His emphasis on the "I" wasn't lost on her. Maria swallowed her doubt. It didn't go down easily. He sounded so sure, but she'd seen what Martin did to people who stood in the way of what he wanted.

The woman who stood first in line approached. Maria recognized her from town. She was one of the wives of the Alamo soldiers. "Please, Señora, help my child." Maria's breath caught at the use of the honorific. Did the know she'd run away from her husband? But the woman's eyes shifted to George and Maria. The formal title for a married woman was because George was there. Maria gave herself a brief second to try on the thought of being married to George. It was a good thought. A *right* thought.

The mother was talking: "She has a terrible cough and I can do nothing to get rid of it. She has stopped eating, and I am so afraid she will…" The woman swallowed hard, and instead of finishing her worry simply held the infant out for Maria. Maria took her and looked down at the sleeping face. Her cheeks were bright with fever.

Maria looked up at George and nodded. "I will try," Maria said to the mother. Maria turned and went back into the house. George followed and shut the door behind her. Before the door shut Maria saw the mother fall to her knees in the dirt in fervent prayer and the noise of the crowd resumed, people begging her to heal their loved ones. In the relative quiet of the house she leaned her back against the door and took deep breaths, trying to ignore the muttering din of the crowd outside.

Maria carried the infant to a rocking chair near the one window in the small living room. The infant was too hot in her arms. She coughed a little. It was a pitiful, weak sound. Maria unwrapped the blanket from the tiny child revealing a homespun white dress. The infant's chubby arms immediately puckered in gooseflesh and she shivered.

"Can you help her?" George approached, his eyes shimmering as he gazed on the ill baby.

"I think so. I have to try."

"What do you need me to do?" He was so earnest in his question, Maria could not make him leave the room.

"Just sit," she said pointing to a chair opposite her own. "Don't talk."

George sat. He leaned forward, his elbows on his knees, hands clasped as though in prayer. Prayers would not hurt right now, Maria thought.

Maria shut her eyes and pushed away the thought of George watching her and of the line of people outside. This infant needed her help, and George was safe. She sent up her own prayer. *God, let him be safe. Let him not be like Martin.*

Maria rocked the infant and hummed the song her mother had sung to her. She found the tune. Far away, she heard George's sharp indrawn breath and knew it was working. She held the infant tighter as she rocked and sang her song to the little girl. The infant's breathing evened out. Maria continued singing. Only when the song was over did she open her eyes. The baby girl gazed at her, brown eyes wide and fascinated.

"Hello, little one," Maria said, stroking one soft cheek with the back of her finger. The baby girl cooed and smiled a toothless smile up at Maria. Maria laughed and snuggled the girl to her face. Her skin was cool against Maria's cheek with no trace of the terrible fever she'd had only minutes ago.

"That's incredible," George said. Maria smiled at him, relieved. George stood and walked to her. He gently placed his large hand on the infant's fore-

head. "No fever. She was blazing hot when you brought her in."

"The secret is out, George" Maria said, reality settling. She folded the blanket over the infant. "Martin will find me now." She looked down at the smiling infant girl and ran a hand over the soft curls capping her head. "I should leave."

"But you won't," George said. Maria heard the question in his voice and shook her head.

"No. Not this time."

"Motherhood looks good on you," George said, and Maria felt her cheeks heat.

"I have to give her back," she said dodging the topic. She stood and opened the door. When she handed the infant to her mother, the woman gave a cry of joy. She wept and wrapped her free arm around Maria, the infant pressed between them. Maria took the thanks with a murmur. The crowd picked up on this and burst out with cries for Maria to see their loved one next. Maria gestured to the next person in line, a man holding up his injured wife, one arm cradled in a makeshift sling. She brought the woman inside and shut the door. No. She would not run this time.

Martin marched his garrison and stationed them outside the Misión San Antonio de Valero. Martin was mildly surprised at the humbleness of the structure. In his mind he'd built it up to be much larger.

"We wait here until General Santa Anna issues further orders," he told his Major General, a neat and capable man who Martin had Maria save the life of more than once. The man was Martin's to his bones. "Tell the men to set up camp. And Major, I expect each of them to be neat and orderly. I will inspect when I return."

The Major nodded and rode off to issue the orders.

Now that that was done, Martin tucked his shotgun under his arm, saddled his horse and headed for the creek. A washer woman would need to be near water.

Maria and George were down by the creek when the attack began. It was a Tuesday afternoon in February. The week had been unseasonably warm, and Maria took this opportunity to earn some extra money. George was on leave from his station at the Misión San Antonio de Valero. George lay back on the bank of the creek chewing a piece of long grass and watching Maria as she waded into the cold water and dunked his clothing.

Maria grumbled at him good naturedly. "Explain to me why I wasted my time teaching you to do this?" Maria stomped up and down on the dirty clothing to get it good and wet.

George took the grass stem from his mouth. "Well, here's the thing. I'm just not as good at it as you are." The laughter in his eyes belied the seriousness of his face. "Besides, I like the scenery." He raised his eyebrows suggestively. Maria laughed and threw a wet shirt at him. The shirt landed at his feet.

"I do believe you meant that for my head." And with that he was off the bank and splashing into the water after her.

Maria shrieked laughter and backed away from him. She lost her balance and sat down hard. The cold water shocked her and she gasped. George laughed, a deep baritone of a sound, and waded in deeper to offer her a hand. Maria took his outstretched hand, bit her lip playfully and George's eyes widened with realization just before she yanked as hard as she could. The desired effect was achieved, and he splashed down into the water beside her. He came up drenched and spluttering. Maria rocked with laughter. George sat up in the water beside her, hip to hip so he was facing the other bank of the creek.

"Well, I guess these clothes are clean now too," he said. Maria's laughter died away, though the occasional giggle bubbled up. The day was hot and the water cool. They sat there in comfortable silence, both lost in their own thoughts for a time. Maria watched the dragon flies dancing along the bank of the creek. Maria let her thoughts drift, and as they drifted, she hummed.

George turned to her. "Maria?"

"Mm-hm?" Maria kept humming, enjoying the rich green of the grass, the brighter greens and blues and browns of the dragon flies.

"Will you marry me?"

Maria stopped humming. The colors faded back to normal. She turned to him. "What did you say?"

"You heard me. Will you marry me?"

"George, how can I do that? You know I'm already married."

"No one else knows that. Maria, we could start over. It's been months and he hasn't found you. You're done with him."

"But Martin…" Maria said, but she trailed off. What *about* Martin? She wasn't going back to him, and he hadn't found her. Maybe she was really safe. Maybe she could really start over with this man. With this good, *good* man.

"Maria," George said, taking her hands into his. "I love you. I want to spend the rest of my life with you. I want to give you the children you've always wanted, and the kind of life you don't even know you deserve. I want us to grow old together and watch our grandchildren play in the front yard. I cannot promise I'll never be angry with you, but I can promise I will never hit you. I will never hurt you."

Maria only watched him, the ability of speech abandoning her completely.

"Please say something," he said, red coloring his cheeks. "I don't want to beg."

"Yes," Maria said breathlessly. She couldn't believe she was agreeing to this, and surely it was a sin against God's law, but it felt so right that Maria thought maybe God understood. "Yes, I will marry you."

George's face split into a grin so wide she thought his face must hurt. "Really?"

Maria laughed and splashed water at him. "I just told you yes, didn't I?"

George wrapped his arms around her and pressed the side of her face into his wet shirt. She nuzzled into him, relishing the feel of him so close. She looked up at him and he lowered his lips to hers, kissing her gently at first, then with a wild abandon. When they parted, her lips felt bruised and wanting more.

George looked as breathless as she felt. "When?"

"As soon as possible," Maria said. George grinned and Maria's cheeks heated with how forthright she'd been.

George's entire posture stiffened, and he frowned.

"Or we can wait if you want," Maria said, suddenly hesitant.

"No, do you hear that? That's not right. They shouldn't be ringing so late in the day."

Maria stopped to listen. Sure enough, in the distance she heard the Misión San Antonio de Valero church bells ringing.

Just then a frightened woman burst through the bushes. She grabbed Maria, hissing a string of hurried words in Spanish as she pulled Maria to the road. The conflict between Martin and George was plain, but in the woman's distress she only had eyes for Maria.

"Debes salvar a mi hija, por favor, Señora, debes salvar a mi hijo," she kept repeating in Spanish. You must save my child, please Señora, you must save my child.

"Wait, I can't leave," Maria said. Those bells unsettled her, but she couldn't say why. "I don't want to leave you."

"Go help her," George said, nodding to the woman pawing desperately at Maria's arm. "I'll pull the clothes out and come find you." George frowned in the direction of the Mission. "I don't like those bells. It's too early in the day. I need to find out what's happening."

"But—"

"Maria, I'll find you. Go help her."

Maria nodded and went with the woman, glancing back to George. She couldn't say why but she thought this might be the last time she saw George alive.

"Well, well, well. What do we have here?" Martin Perez emerged from between the dense bushes beside the creek. Slung casually over one arm was a double-barreled shotgun. The tall American was stooped over, hauling heavy wet clothing up and onto the bank. He saw Martin and made as if to go after his gun in the bushes. Martin, quick as a snake, had his own gun up and pointing at the George.

"Tell me, sir, have you been enjoying my wife?"

"You're Martin," George said.

"So, she told you about me. Tell me, before I kill you, where is she?" Martin eyed the wet clothing sardonically. "Or do the men in this country do the woman's work?"

George stood up as straight as he could. The man was tall. He topped Martin's own height by at least half a foot, but the weight of the gun in his hands made up for his missing inches.

"I won't tell you where she is," George said.

"Suit yourself," Martin said and fired. The blast hit the American directly in the middle and he doubled over, then crumpled on the side of the creek

bank. Martin nodded once to himself noting a job well done, then turned and strode away through the bushes in search of his errant wife.

Reluctantly Maria followed the frightened woman. The woman led her to a small house. Inside a boy of about twelve was lying on a thin bed. The boy had a gunshot wound in his stomach. He did not have long to live, and judging by his cramped and sweating features, Maria knew he was in a great deal of pain.

"What happened to him?"

Through the woman's tears Maria caught enough of the story to understand. There had been fighting at the mission and the boy carried a message away to warn the surrounding communities.

"Santa Anna?"

"Sí. Por favor, ayúdelo Señora."

Maria sat down shakily in a chair the woman set beside the bed. The mother stood back wringing her hands, and an almost rabid hopefulness shone in her eyes.

Maria sat down and hummed, but her thoughts were all bent on George and Marin—the song kept slipping away from her. She had to stop and collect her thoughts.

"Por favor, Señora, por favor cante. Por favor, ayúdelo." Please, Señora, please sing. please help him.

"I am trying," Maria said. She took the boy's hand in her own and with effort pushed away all thoughts of what Martin might be doing to George down by the creek. At first the song would not come. In the distance she heard gunfire. The fighting at the mission.

When the gunfire paused, Maria found a moment of peace. Her song came to her then, haltingly at first, but there.

"That's all I can do," Maria said, exhaustion settling over her like a blanket.

"No está despierto." The woman looked confused, worried.

"He still may not wake up. His wound was very bad. Please, I must go. I must find help."

Maria left the mother praying beside her son's bed. He would heal or he would not. She had to go find help for George.

Maria rushed back to the creek as soon as she could pull herself away from the mother.

"George, I'm back," Maria said as she approached the creek. "It was so hard to sing, George, that boy was so hurt. There's something wrong at the mission. There's fighting. I think you should go see—" Maria came around the bend in the path and stopped short.

George was lying on his back on the creek bed, the water rippling around his bare feet. There was a terrible wound in his chest. Blood trailed downstream in a thin rivulet.

"George!" Maria rushed down to the water's edge and put her ear to his chest. There was a very weak heartbeat. "Hold on, George. Just hold on. Don't you leave me."

Maria tried to still herself and find her song. *"Duérmete…mi…niño,"* she began shakily, but the song felt all wrong. Unfamiliar and distant.

A crowd drew in. Families from the nearby community, hiding from the fighting down by the creek, crept from the bushes and scrub brush along the creek. They gathered about Maria, but they couldn't help her and were silent in their helplessness. Husbands held weeping wives. Maria did not see them. Her eyes were only for George and the life she saw slipping away beneath her fingertips.

Maria tried again but her eyes kept popping open and she found herself pawing over George's wounded body. Sobs racked her body. George was fading away from her and she couldn't breathe. She forced herself to concentrate, gathering enough air to make one noise. She wailed her grief and the sound of it was as loud and as raw a noise as anyone had ever heard.

Maria choked with emotion and went silent. She rested her cheek on George's still body, stroking his hair with one hand. Her pain left her hollow and empty.

"I'm sorry, George," she said. Her voice was a husky whisper. "I couldn't do it. I could save everyone except the one who mattered."

She closed her eyes and softly sang another song she'd learned from her mother. She sang it because it was a song of lost love, of heartbreak too heavy to bear. And she sang it because it didn't matter what song she sang now. George was gone from her. Maria poured all of her love and grief and hurt into each note.

She didn't hear the indrawn breaths or the murmurs of the crowd all around her. She only knew she had to sing this song, or she would die of heartbreak. A warm, strong hand stroked her hair and she sat up with a jerk. George was looking up at her.

Maria's tears fell on George's chest. She pulled back his shirt and gasped. His wound was knit shut.

"But how? I couldn't sing the song," she said. "I'm sorry, I couldn't sing. But you're here. How?"

"It was never the song, Maria," George said. His voice was husky and tired, as though after a long illness. "It was always the love you sang the song with. It was always that."

A boy ran up to Maria. He started babbling to her so fast in Spanish even Maria couldn't keep up.

"Slow down, please," Maria said. The boy's father stepped up beside him.

"He says a man came looking for you. A Mexican soldier."

"Martin," Maria said. "Where is he now?"

"He is gone, Señora. Sent back to the mission."

The boy grinned. "We told him you'd gone there looking for him."

Martin rode back to the mission. The boy had said she went looking for him. Good. He had a few lessons to teach her. One of which was about running away. Another was about monogamy. Martin arrived at the mission, and the battle was raging. The Texians had socked themselves away inside the mission, firing at Santa Anna's army. Martin's own men were among those firing back.

Someone, Martin couldn't tell who, yelled an alarm when Martin approached, and the guns turned on him. Several shots zipped past his head and peppered the ground at his horse's feet.

"I am one of your officers," he said in the most commanding voice he could muster, but he was drowned out by the chaos of the battle. Martin dismounted. More shots fired in his direction and he hid behind the bulk of his horse. The horse whinnied and eyes rolled in fear. Martin's heart pounded. The fools were going to kill him!

"Hold your fire!"

The firing ceased for a moment and Martin peeked around his horse. The fighting with the Texians had lulled and Martin saw his chance. He came out from behind the horse and held his hands up.

"I am one of your officers. My name is Martin Perez."

A voice came from the crowd. "I know who you are." The private with the scraggly beard, the one who had told him where to look for Maria in the first place, stood and held his gun pointed at Martin.

Martin exhaled in relief. "Put that down you idiot," Martin said, "before I have you whipped for disobeying an officer of Santa Anna's army."

The private did not lower his weapon and Martin felt a thread of unease work through his belly. Martin looked at the faces of the men surrounding the private. They all wore grim expressions, and Martin suddenly understood they knew what they were doing.

"I won't be whipped again," the private said, and fired his gun. The shot took Martin in the left side of his chest and he sank to his knees in the hard-packed dirt. Martin put his hand to his chest where he'd been shot. It came away bloody. He fell over, his cheek in the dirt, his eyes still full of the surprise that those he'd abused would fight back.

The men of Santa Anna's army won the battle of the Alamo. The men of Martin Perez's unit never spoke of how their commanding officer came to be shot on the battleground. Martin Perez was listed among the casualties of the day, and his name became a mere footnote on the pages of history.

By turn of luck, George Kimble was mistakenly listed among the dead that day at what later was known as the Battle of the Alamo. His name can be found on the memorial wall in San Antonio, Texas. Maria is not mentioned in the history books. The community that lived by the creek knew the truth, but they never corrected the mistake. They said nothing when George Kimble and Maria Perez quietly, and with no fanfare, became Charles and Mary Kimble. Their four children and twelve grandchildren, who were later born and raised in the same community, were taught by their mothers and their grandmother the story of the miracles the love of one woman brought. To this day, the creek beside which Maria found her true power is still known as Woman Hollering Creek.

Copyright © 2019 by Meghan Ewald.

Multiple award-winning author, Jacqueline Seewald, has taught creative, expository and technical writing at Rutgers University as well as high school English. She also worked as both an academic librarian and an educational media specialist. Nineteen of her books of fiction have been published to critical praise including books for adults, teens and children. Her most recent novels are Death Promise *and* Witch Wish. *Her short stories, poems, essays, reviews and articles have appeared in hundreds of diverse publications and numerous anthologies such as:* The Writer, L.A. Times, Reader's Digest, Pedestal, Sherlock Holmes Mystery Magazine, Over My Dead Body!, Gumshoe Review, Library Journal, Publishers Weekly *and* The Christian Science Monitor. *She enjoys painting landscapes and singing along to all kinds of music. Her writer's blog can be found at: http://jacquelineseewald.blogspot.com.*

JUST ONE LOOK

by Jacqueline Seewald

We were sitting at poolside when I decided to test the inviting aqua water. Suddenly a beach ball whizzed by.

"Sorry," came an abashed apology, "I meant to send it into your hands."

I blinked. Standing not far from me was the handsomest man I'd ever seen. His tan was accentuated by sun-streaked hair and he had the body of Michelangelo's *David*. I let out an appreciative sigh.

"That's all right," I said, tossing the ball back to him. I hoped my mouth wasn't gaping, as I knew it wasn't my most alluring pose.

"Mind if I join you?" he asked.

I minded about as much as having someone offer me a winning lottery ticket.

"I'm Todd Driscoll," he said.

After a brief pause, I finally remembered my name. "Rosemary Jenkins."

"So is this your first cruise, Rosemary?" He had very intense eyes, velvet brown in color like rich Swiss chocolate.

I realized I was staring and caught myself. "Yes, first time on a cruise ship. You too?"

He smiled and I saw a dimple twinkling in his right cheek. "My friend talked me into going. He insisted we'd have a good time."

"And are you?"

"Having a good time? Well, I wasn't, but I think that's going to change." He gave me a meaningful look. "So who or what made you decide on a Caribbean cruise?"

"I too came with a friend. Karen and I work together. We're both nurses."

By this time, Karen joined us. Todd charmed both my girlfriend and me. We found out he was a graduate of Kansas University who had majored in math and physics. He had come back to New York full of idealism and taught math, working in special services schools to help the most needy students. He told us that he was a vegetarian and half convinced us to become vegan ourselves. Finally, we left to get ready for the evening. Todd said he would look for us at dinner.

"Quite a guy," Karen observed as we selected our dresses.

"He is very attractive."

Karen twirled a lock of auburn hair around her finger. "Love at first sight?" she teased.

I wasn't going down that road. I'd just met Todd. I hardly knew him at all. However, I took extra time and care with my appearance.

Looks aren't everything as far as I'm concerned. I don't consider myself a superficial or shallow person. But I admit the first thing I notice about the opposite sex is what the guy looks like. If there's no physical attraction, no chemical reaction, it's not likely the relationship is going beyond friendship.

When we got to the dining room, I didn't see Todd and felt disappointed. We seated ourselves and I perused the menu; although, I wasn't much interested in food at that moment. The waiter handed me a second menu.

"I already have one," I said, thinking he was overdoing the service. Like how big a tip was he expecting?

"This is from the gentleman over there." He pointed to a young man wearing dark-rimmed glasses dressed in a neat conservative suit.

At the top of the menu, I found something handwritten: "Girls who wear glasses do get passes." The paraphrase of Dorothy Parker seemed cryptic. I admit I do have mild astigmatism, but I prefer not to wear glasses except when it's absolutely necessary. Maybe it is a form of vanity.

After dinner, Todd came over and asked if I would join him for the evening. He made certain to introduce Karen to his friend, Jim. Tall, slender and easy-going, Jim made an immediately favorable impression on Karen. And so we became a friendly foursome.

Before we took seats in the nightclub, Todd asked if I preferred to sit up front for the show. "I figure you don't see very well. You walked right past me before dinner without saying a word. You didn't recognize me, did you?"

"No, but you look different with your clothes on." I felt my face turn red. "You weren't wearing glasses at the pool," I added quickly.

Todd smiled. "I always use contact lenses and goggles when I go swimming. I wear glasses the rest of the time. So don't be embarrassed to wear yours."

"How can you be so certain I wear glasses?"

"Just a hunch," he said.

"Well, I do have eyeglasses," I admitted. "I'm slightly near-sighted. But I only need glasses occasionally."

"I only wear mine to see," he said with a wry grin.

"Okay, I guess I could wear mine," I conceded. With that, I whipped my glasses out of my evening bag.

"I like the look," he assured me.

As we watched the show, I realized that I found Todd just as attractive now as I had earlier in the day, although his appearance was somewhat different.

The more we spoke, the more I got to like him. Todd was not only handsome outside but inside where it counted most.

Our itinerary promised exotic locations. We were sailing the Western Caribbean. We toured the islands together with Karen and Jim.

In the Mexican port of Cozumel, we decided to take a cab into town and from there go snorkeling. Diving gear was provided and a crewman led our group off a reef. Beneath the ocean were spectacular drop-offs, walls and swim-throughs, beautiful coral gardens where we observed large pelagic fish and dolphins. It seemed as if the fish were lit up by neon lights, their colors brilliant and iridescent.

After returning to the downtown, we had lunch at a small restaurant decorated with Mayan artifacts. The area was packed with colorful shops, markets and tourists. Then we walked to a lagoon reserve full of turtles surrounded by a botanical garden.

"I love the hibiscus and other tropical flowers," I said as we walked through the garden.

"So you love brightly colored flowers," Todd said.

"What woman doesn't?"

As we left the gardens, Todd stopped by a street vendor, selected a bouquet and handed it to me. "For the brightest flower of all who puts the rest to shame."

I think I must have blushed as bright pink as the hibiscus. Okay, maybe the line was a tad corny, but Todd made me feel like a princess in a fairy tale.

Later we caught a tour bus. The Punta Celarin Lighthouse had a mystical quality. There was extraordinary music produced by wind whistling through the encrusted shells of the walls. It made me shiver with an odd longing.

"This is a place for the ghosts of long dead lovers to meet," Todd whispered in my ear.

I shook my head at him. "You read too much Stephen King."

The boyish dimple winked in his cheek. "My mother accuses me of having an overactive imagination."

"Who am I to disagree with a man's mom?"

It was funny how well we hit it off, how easy the conversation was between us. We could talk about nothing and everything. Even the silences were companionable.

At Grand Cayman Island, we decided to go snorkeling again. The water was warm, with very little current. At the edge of a coral reef in ten to twenty feet of water, we saw reef fish, coral heads and a huge, green moray eel. Unfortunately, we also saw sharks.

Todd indicated them, then led me protectively away. I loved the way he watched out for me. I was already half in love with the guy.

Our next stop was Sting Ray City. Here the water was only three to four feet deep and the rays numerous. We were provided with squid to feed the rays and carefully instructed how to go about it. The rays were like big cats, rubbing up against me, nuzzling my back and legs.

"I think I'm getting jealous here," Todd said. The next thing I knew, he was imitating the rays.

"Stop!" I ended up giggling like a schoolgirl. Todd made it clear in every possible way that he found me attractive. He saw me as a beautiful woman. I never saw myself that way until I met him. I truly loved his perception of me.

We had a fish lunch at the harbor front where Karen admired the gingerbread-style buildings lining the area. When the guys left us for a few minutes, Karen turned to me.

"You and Todd really look good together. This appears to be more than a mere vacation romance."

"Could be," I agreed. "But I don't know for certain."

"Why not?"

I didn't answer my friend. I knew I was attracted to Todd, but would our relationship actually turn into something more meaningful?

On the surface, everything appeared perfect—or would have been except for one thing: Todd's fixation about me wearing my glasses. He kept reminding me to put them on and even teased me about being vain. It flat-out annoyed me. I began to have some doubts. Maybe Todd wasn't so terrific after all.

I tried to ignore those disturbing thoughts. At Ocho Rios, Jamaica, we stayed with a tour group for a trip to Fern Gully and the Botanical Gardens, with the final stop at Dunn's River Falls.

I enjoyed the lush Botanical Gardens. "I've never seen anything more beautiful," I said with a sigh.

"Well, there's seeing and then there's really seeing," Todd said. "Imagine how much more incredible it would be if you didn't have to squint myopically. Why don't you put on your glasses?"

It was just too much. Not the lecture again! Ugh, I hated it. "What next? Are you going to sing a chorus of *You're So Vain*?"

"Maybe I should."

"I wish you'd stop nagging me. You're spoiling everything. I'm beginning to see you all too clearly without my glasses and it's not an attractive sight." With that, I stalked back to the bus and proceeded to ignore Todd. Sure, I realized I'd hurt his feelings, but at the moment I was too angry to care.

Karen tried to talk to me when we reached our final stop at the waterfall, but I shook my head and walked away from her and Jim.

"Many tourists climb the falls from the beach right to the top," our native guide explained. "They stop on the way to enjoy the cool plunge pools in the river rocks. But I should mention the falls are steep and slippery."

"We'll skip it then," Todd said, stepping in beside me.

I was still mad at him. He had no right to arbitrarily make decisions for me. So I joined those who chose to explore the waterfall. The water flowed like buttermilk making the steps hard to see. But once I began, there was no turning back. The water rushed fast, pounding and swirling. It was difficult to tell where I was putting my feet. I couldn't see beneath the surface.

As I lost my balance, I realized I'd made a dumb decision. Terrified, I was certain I was going to fall to my death! Suddenly, Todd was there with me. He caught me up and held me tightly in his arms. I buried my face against his chest.

"How did you know I was in trouble?" I asked in a breathless voice.

"X-ray vision, of course." The irresistible smile had returned.

"No I-told-you-so?"

"Nope, and no more nagging either. I'm sorry for that. I meant well. Didn't see that I was irritating you." He caressed my cheek and kissed my hand. "Do what you want from now on. Just promise not to plunge off any waterfalls."

"I think we can agree on that. You might say we basically see things the same way after all."

I realized that I'd been too sensitive about wearing my glasses. In a moment of clear insight, I recognized that I had behaved childishly, acting vain about my appearance.

Todd studied me thoughtfully as if he were reading my mind. "You're beautiful in my eyes whether you wear glasses or not."

And that was when I did see clearly for the first time and realized that I was falling in love with Todd.

Copyright © 2004 by Jacqueline Seewald.

Rei Rosenquist is a queer agender (they/them) speculative and contemporary fiction writer who depicts a wide variety of identities struggling to find a place in a wide variety of worlds. They are also a lifelong barista, baker, and nomad. Over the years, they have traveled to many countries, engaged many peoples, picked up new habits, and learned new languages. But, some things never change. For them, the constants of life are made up of love stories, great coffee, delicious food, and traveling. Rei's work can be found in previous Heart's Kiss issues, Enter the Aftermath *by TANSTAAFL Press,* Beauty & Wickedness *by Blackbird Publishing, and* Midwinter Fae *by Blackbird Publishing. You can also find more of Rei's work by visiting their website reirosenquist.com. Stay in touch by connecting via Facebook (Rei Rosenquist), Instagram (@rylrosenquist) and Twitter (@ rylrosenquist).*

A REAL ACE V-DAY PRESENT

by Rei Rosenquist

The City is preparing for V-Day.

Along the Wall sits a four-stories tall solid black composite-fiber structure that divides the city into two concentric circles. Colorful garlands swing in a breeze that isn't yet as cold as it will become V-Day past. People mistakenly think Xmas is the coldest day of the year. Wrong. It's V-Day. And not just weatherly speaking. Those with lovers are ever-fated to do the holiday all wrong. And those without lovers are constantly reminded how none of this is for them.

Inside the Wall, humans wear their pink and purple heart-shaped fuzzy mufflers in preparation of the holiday. They sip fresh-made cocoa lattes with winky face sprinkles and lazily stroll, hand in mittened hand, down Restaurant Row. Nobody makes eye contact with lovers or strangers alike, all too busy checking personal mailz on their glittery hand-held devices.

Outside the Wall, par-humans sit in offices, box-like row after row of consoles, sipping cocoa rip-off beverages that taste saccharine and bile-bitter at the same time. Their part-carbon, part-silicon backs are bent working without breaks on the adi-V-scans that'll make big bucks for the big Corps come the stupid cupid holiday rush.

Beyond the City is nothing. A desolate landscape. The City is all that's left of a world torn apart. And right now, V-Day is all the City cares about. A singular holiday in a singular world.

In the Mall, the singular shopping district open only to those who can afford to spend a little something on their sweetheart, the piped in "fresh-baked" smell of pink pies and heart-shaped cookies fill the air, blown down from heavy-duty machine Perfumators set up in the rafters.

The same old cheeze lovey-dovey tunes written hundreds of years ago by the venerated Lovers of Old fill the radio waves of everyone's personal auditory services, rich or poor. Pale blue, warm pink, and soft lavender string lights sparkle from shop windows stocked full of the most invasive scanners loaded with the most intrusive adi-V-scans ready to grab each and every passerby. Each adi-V-scan is hand-tailored by a par-human for each and every individual.

"Buy your sweetheart a brand-new Woolly Warm Coat and they'll be warm all winter!" takes the warm-blooded human slant.

"Get yourself a fresh EZ Glide Paint Coat and prevent rusty lock up where it counts!" takes the par-human perspective with a robo-winky face.

"Got a ho-hum lonely par-human maître d? Get vem a GooberGoodie Playstation programmed to keep their sorrows at bay! Works only during official work breaks!" Human rich.

"Got debt yah can't beat? Get yourself a heart-shaped BeatItTM Punching Bag to relieve undo stress this holiday!" Par-human poor.

Oh. Such holiday spirit in the air for Valentine, mascot of lovers everywhere. A celebration made up of relentless marketing trying to sell every heart-shaped thing ever made.

I avoid the worst adi-V-scans from picking me out of the body-flood by aiming my inline skates a good distance from any window shop. These inlines might be majorly biffed up from all the time they've seen in the derby rink, but they still do a fine job. I cruise smoothly down the center boulevard of the deep-end pavilion where all the V-Day early-outers from work are oogling pink heart-shaped junk for their loves.

In a shop window, I see two jerseys side by side. The colors are my old team. Electric blue and white with purple polka dots. One jersey reads "Blue Jay 101" and the other reads "granJan 701"

An adi-V-scan flashes across my vision.

"Get your fave fan logos here! Best in Trouny! Best in Derby! The Once Great ResistiRollers!"

Not a real ace reminder, that. I feel all torn up in three seconds flat.

I use a quick hack to delete the adi-V-scan's permission to contact me. Tears wet the corners of my eyes. I lie and tell myself it's from the wind. But, I'm not rolling that fast. Then, as if reality wants to make a point, I hit another sudden blue light. I screech to a halt and dash my eyes dry.

I can't help but thinking back to that day, our last skate. granJan had been on fire. Like vey were preparing for something big. We didn't win that rally, though. There'd been this huge riot going on in the Pavilion outside the Gate. Par-humans getting mowed down like grass by Gate guards. It was all over the feeds.

"This is what happens when you try to break society," the human newsfeeds claimed.

Thin argument.

Maybe humans hold all the physical keys to the City, but par-humans are the gatekeepers of the City's infrastructure deep programming. Even your run-of-the-mill adi-V-scans are written by people like me. Part human, part android lifeforms who have more silicone in their bodies than carbon. Par-human brains process massive amounts of meta-data per second. We whip out all the stuff that keeps the City afloat like an afterthought.

More like: this is what happens when the oppressed try to get an even break.

We all felt the riots at the Pavilion in our bones. Everyone was off their game. We lost and went home, beat. Most of us got up the next day and carried on.

granJan never came back.

Everyone knows what happened. Even without any newsfeed reports or a dead body.

Happens all the time.

I blast off the curb, burning my sorrow by pumping extra hard. Just like I used to do in the rink. I hit a hard right and fly down the weaving twist of back-way streets. I pass lowgrade shop after lowgrade shop full of kitschy V-Day stuff. In darkened alcoves, massive armored Road Rovers lay in wait, geared up for the coming snow with tires wrapped in thick chains to beat the slush and muck.

One upside. To make way for the Rovers' exodus, the usual heaps of trash that line the curbs and make for a brutal obstacle course have been all cleared away. So getting into the middle of the road is easy-peasy skating. I zone out, trying to think of nothing at all.

Not derby. Not granJan. Not how utterly desolate this V-Day is gonna be once it comes.

Nothing.

I come out into the main avenue just as a traffic light in front of me changes from gold for go to blue for stop. I see it too late, skid on my breaks and swerve hard toward the sidewalk.

A huge pack of bag-laden shoppers surge into the crosswalk. I try to elbow-pad my way through the mess, but the bodies keep coming. Pushing, shoving. One of the humans trips me with a mean glint in their hot pink and seafoam green eyes, I fall to the left, my inline whizzes to the right, and down I'm going toward the gray unforgiving concrete.

I hear something crack before my hands hit the ground.

A loud horn blasts in my ears. I barely have time to tuck and roll before a Road Rover, out ahead of schedule, comes chugging past me. I face-plant in the middle of the intersection. Eat a bloody mouthful of concrete. I roll onto my side, both hands oozing pale yellow liquid.

Good ol' Fluxx Fluid, a saline-based liquid that flows through my body like blood and auto-fixes holes in my system like super-fast super glue. Only two problems. One: when it's working hard and fast, it smells so awful I want to gag. Two: it makes it duxing hard to move.

The huge chunky metal-wrapped wheels rattle by, shaking my brain-shell.

Once it's gone, I sit up sloggishly. With a pit of dread in my stomach, I examine my throbbing ankle.

Well, that's a win. Nothing snapped or shorting out as far as I can tell. Bruised, but Fluxx Fluid will get that patched up soon. All I've got to do is skate myself to the curb and wait.

All in all, a lucky no-break.

I check the status of my inlines to see if they're still roll-able or not. Bad news. One of the wheels on my left skate has popped loose, cracked in half, rolled its last.

Well, dux. Doesn't this suck.

The light ahead of me goes from gold to blue and traffic slows to a stop, waiting for me to get the dux outta the road. I stand shakily, but before I can make any headway toward the curb, my busted skate skids and freezes up, leaving a black mark where I just was. I tumble sideways and crack my knee pad hard against the concrete. I groan and huff, knowing I'll have to wait in the middle of the street for the Fluxx Fluid to taper off so I can move properly.

I count down how long I have.

Fifteen, fourteen, thirteen.

Someone approaches me from the opposite curb, and I assume it's some wisecrack on a whizz-board about to tell me to get my loser skate-clad self out the intersection before the light changes. Don't I know it, asspass!

Or maybe it'll be the Copper Pops—as in human cops—here to kick my bruised face in or taze me while shouting at me to move, depending on their current mood.

The sound of feet clomp-tromping stops right beside me.

Here we go.

Something fleshy touches my shoulder. Despite how wet and weird human flesh is, the light pressure and velvet-soft texture is oddly reassuring. I look up through my tinted goggles, steel eyes wide.

"You look…could…" says the flesh-and-blood human with real vocal chords.

The vibrating sounds are so strange that I barely recognize the language as my own. Most likely, whatever they said—it's rude. I swat the plump hand away, go to stand, and flail gracelessly. My one working skate whizzes out from under me again, and I crash down on my ass.

"Ow," I groan.

"Here, lemme help," the human says again, and this time all the sounds register as words.

"I-uh-yeah-thanks," I mutter, leaning on the human's arm to regain my balance.

My knee twitches, but I ignore it. Good ol' Fluxx Fluid will get it working soon.

The human helps me skuttle to the curb. We sit side by side, and the human hands me a towel to soak up the stanky excess Fluxx Fluid dripping down my wrists. I wipe it away quick and dispose of the towel. Then I reach down and take my skates off. With a sad sigh, I tuck them under my arm. How I'm gonna get that busted wheel fixed? If only I could Fluxx Fluid it.

If only my old team leader, granJan, were here to tell me what to do.

No such luck. granJan up and disappeared over a year ago. No body found. I could use my imagination, but I'd rather not. The skates, like granJan, are probably a goner. I'll have to chuck them soon.

I can't bring myself to do it here on a street corner. I tuck them under my arm for safe keeping.

"You gonna keep those?" human asks.

I glare up into the human's face, lean in mean and close until we're nose-to-nose.

And whoa.

What a cute nose it is. Covered in porous melanin-rich flesh the color of fresh compost—a color I can't remember the last time I saw in nature. It's too alive for this world. Yet here it is, before my eyes. Downy hair, long as a whip, caught up in a soft braid so shimmery it could be made of pure copper.

Brown eyes. Not the bold violet-blue or hush lavender and gold-green, not even the velvety sunrise violet-pink of humanity these days. Those colors are all made-up, CRISPR genetic cocktails you can add on (not for cheap). But brown is free because "brown is mundane, and mundane is ugly."

So adi-V-scans all claim.

But the adi-V-scans all lie because these eyes aren't brown like wet cardboard box or shit swirling in the bottom of a dirty porto. These eyes are perfect wooden marbles made back when there was real wood and real artisans to make art out of it. Each orb is framed beautifully by thin copper eyebrows and set into a smooth, high brow.

I could get lost in these eyes, wander in their living woods, and never come back home.

Some cheezeball V-Day writer once said, "The human eye is the window to the human heart."

And I used to think it was just more human versus par-human trash. But now I'm thinking I was wrong. Because these eyes are breath-taking cliffs, and I've inadvertently stumbled off the ledge into somebody else.

"What's it to you?" I mumble to hide all the woo-woo oozy crush junk I'm thinking.

"Nothing," Human says and leans away from me.

I cradle my skates and shift my weight, hanging around for some reason I can't explain.

Actually, I can. I'm intrigued by this human who stopped to help me up, and I don't want to walk away just yet. Dumb as that is. To stall, I introduce myself.

"I'm Blue Jay." I barely manage to stick to my business-only name.

"Nice to meet you," the human says, voice softening into a level mid-range voice that's both nondescript and, for that very reason, intoxicating. I can't even pin down this human's sex or gender, which is odd. Unique. That fact makes me even more intrigued.

Interested.

Infatuated.

In love?

Whoa, no. I must be letting all this V-Day gunk clog up my head. All the adi-V-scans babbling inside my thoughts. "Get a lover" and "Buy 'em candy!" and so on. It's too much. I'm losing my nerve.

"My name's Razor Fade," the delightfully androgynous human says.

"I assume that's a fake," I say flatly.

Humans don't have names like that. They have boring binary-gendered mythology-based names. John or Mary, Bethel or Jesus, and so on. Even for a login, "Razor Fade" has the wrong ring to it for a blood-and-bones. It sounds like a par-human experiment gone wrong.

"So is yours," Razor Fade snarks back.

A flutter flits through my belly, and for a second I can't tell if it's fear of Razor Fade being some secret undercover Copper Pop or if it's me thinking Razor Fade is super cool in a way-too-gritty-for-you way.

Razor Fade grins back at me all sly-like. Like this flesh-and-blood knows what I'm thinking. Instead of getting angry, the fluttering in my wires gets flutterier. A gear whirring fast with zero resistance—that's what love feels like inside of me. And it's whirring when I look at RF here, faster and smoother than I'd like.

Shizzle fizzle! No!

I *cannot* fall for a true human.

Major socio-economic status issues. Dangerous power dynamics. Problematic social situations. Not to mention, what happens when fleshie here wants to have sex? Me, being out of the question in all ways: body, heart, and mind. But let's say just for piss and giggles that it did all *somehow* work out. What about all that blood pumping through a heart with holes in it? Seriously limited time offer. I'd just be asking for the hurts.

No. No. No!

From all possible angles, it's bad.

"Welp, that's my name," I say without a hint of a smile.

"Business it is then," RF says, nodding knowingly.

Too knowingly.

The flutter of attraction turns back into a stab of panic so strong it slices through my whole body. Nobody is supposed to know "Blue Jay" is business-only. The only ones outside of granJan who should know that are the adi-V-scans. And that's only because adi-V-scans read direct from internal bar codes. I've made sure that's private personal intel only.

Double-aggressive Virus-Shot protected against prying minds.

So how does RF here know that so certainly? Unless they're from the big inside, AKA Copper Stomps. The meanest of human cops. The fleshbag jackholes who work directly for The Man.

The Man isn't even one of either us, human or par-human.

The Man is a governmental AI piece of shizzle fizzle that runs all the codes of the City. He keeps the Gate closed. He keeps the Wall guards armed and dangerous. He keeps the holidays like V-Day happily segregated by offering huge incentives for companies. He sucks up all that was once good, chews it up, and spits it out in the shape of a cheap trash society nobody actually wants.

The Man was created a hundred years ago by a tiny twisted group of old oppressive oligarchs at the top of the biggest companies in the City.

Today The Man still runs everything because nobody has ever tried to dismantle Him.

Most people don't even believe He actually exists.

But I'm a hacker when I'm not skating, so I know better. I've run directly into His codes and how nastily they work. Missed a whole tourny one year thanks to it. granJan said I had best be more careful, so after that I've avoided The Man like a post-apoc viral wave.

And here I am, talking to an agent of The Man because they've got a sweet voice and pretty eyes? Ugh! What the dux is wrong with me?

I frown with a stiff lip. "I gotta jet. Have a great V-Day, skin-bin."

RF sighs. "Blue Jay, don't go."

I freeze up at that plaintive statement. Blunt, to the point. I want you here. I shiver because I both like the feeling of desire and am pretty sure it's a trap.

"Why?"

"I have a gift for you," RF says, and gives me *that* look. The one humans give to par-humans who they think they are going to save from the slums.

I snap up, glaring. "Oh, so I'm a charity case now? Is that it? You think you can just stroll out of your slick-ass office, find some busted up par-human, offer your hand, and bam! There you have it. Your whole V-Day self-promotion package ready to go? RF, the human who helps the down-and-out par-humans get a hand up. Not a hand out! Double-click for a free date!"

I scoff and spit onto the concrete. "You disgust me."

RF gives me a shrug. "That's a horrible scheme. Besides, I've already helped you off the street," RF says matter-of-fact.

I'm about to go full fire-rage when RF winks.

I blink.

"Oh come on. That was a joke."

Oh. The street. As in, the *actual* street. It's a joke.

"Har har," I spit, but catch myself really laughing. Dux. I haven't laughed since...well, since granJan was alive.

"Okay, okay." I gain my composure. "But why me?"

"Why not? Come on. It's almost V-Day. Can't a human want to be nice?"

I almost say "not without strings attached" but then I catch myself. I think about the coming loneliness of this junk-ass holiday. I think of how much I miss granJan and the team who broke up over the loss of vem. I think about how I haven't spent an evening outside of the charging dock in...in...dux I don't remember. But suddenly taking a risk on a human who wants to be nice to me doesn't feel like the worst thing in the universe.

In fact, it sounds kind of nice.

"Fine. I'll bite."

"Great!" RF smiles too wide to be fake. "Now, before we get going can I ask you something?"

I freeze up, shoulders to my ears. That question has greasy Copper Stomp all over it.

"What are your pronouns?" RF asks like a tool.

I glare cross at those sweet brown eyes. "What the dux do you think? Vey/vem/veir like every other par-human, you asspass."

RF turns a color in the face that makes me uncomfortable. The prickly flush pale but red color of too much blood pooling right underneath the skin.

"Oh shizzle. Sorry. I uh, well, ah, mine are, um, they/them/their," RF babbles foolishly, adding after a long awkward pause, "I'm eh…non-binary, uh, well actually agender specifically. And umm… asexual too. And…oh shizzle. I'm sorry, this is outta control awkward. Shizzle me…"

I blink, my processors all whirring.

Ooooh. I get it.

RF wasn't trying to be an insensitive human-centric jackhole. They were trying to use the question as an in. To start a conversation about *their* identity. Thinking that after I supplied mine, I'd ask theirs in return. And we'd have this interesting conversation about the similarities and differences between a human who happens to be born asexual and a par-human who is by ultimate design.

Complex and complicated conversation that'd be, but interesting.

All things considered it's a clever tactic—*when you're dealing with other humans.*

Graceless and demeaning when addressing a par-human who doesn't have any other option. But RF doesn't seem to know that. I take one look at their down-turned brown eyes, full of obvious regret, and I give them a pass.

"It's fine. Clumsy and short-sighted, but fine."

Then I stop and micro-frown at myself.

"What's wrong?" RF asks carefully.

I wave the question away. The problem is complicated. Because I can't understand why I'm trying to patch things up with a human, of all beings in the known universe.

Humans haven't exactly done my kind a service or anything. More like ruined our lives.

Created The Man to oppress us, left us with the junk-end of the City, punished us brutally for trying

to end segregation once our sentience could be proven in their court rooms, treated us like slaves and thieves. Gangs of humans daily pick us off for fun in the backway alleys of the Outside, the par-human low-budg side of the Wall. They sell our body parts for high prices at silicone and rare metal salvage pawn shops Inside the Wall.

That's why I know what happened to granJan that horrible night.

It wasn't the first time I'd lost someone. Just the closest to my heart.

And yet, here I stand trying to play nice with a human.

"I'm sorry," RF says into my bitter silence. "I'm being a jackhole, aren't I? I've made you feel bad."

I start. That's the first time I've ever heard a human willing to take the blame for anything. It's refreshing, but it can't undo hundreds of years of oppression, can it?

I don't know.

"Why don't you let me grab us a bite?" RF suggests into more silence from me. Still trying instead of walking away.

It's kind of admirable, RF's insistence to keep talking to me. Kind of…adorable.

In a flash, those pesky warm butterflies, the kind I like, are back. Which is bad. I need a good excuse. An exit plan. A way to get lost before all these fluttery butterflies get the better of me.

I pat my belly. "Not hungry."

RF looks down, legit disappointed. "Too bad. My gift to you was gonna be a stub to get into Hacker Haven. I have two, and no one to go with."

See-through as this plot twist is, my eyes still bug out of my skull. Cartoon 3-D zoom-in as my jaw legit hits the floor. Because unlike other mythological haven-like places that don't actually exist (heaven, nirvana, pie in the sky, take your pick), Hacker Haven is a real place.

It's the most famous joint in all of the City. Inside and Outside.

The food, rumor has it, is so rich and real that you don't have to eat for a whole week after one single meal. There, tomatoes are red, blueberries are blue, and every taste will razzle dazzle you! Bread tastes like more than rain-soaked cardboard. There is fresh coffee. The real bean juice. Caffeine, fully intact.

Some people even claim it's the secret home to a last hold-out resistance clan.

As foolish as it legit is, I genuinely want to go.

And, even more foolish, the idea of going with this gooey hunk of a flesh-bag RF doesn't sound half-bad.

The grin on RF's unavoidably pretty face says they know it. It's the ultimate date. Ahem, *offer*. It's the end-all, be-all of outings. A real ace place. The most ace in the whole of the City. A place I'd most certainly never ever get to on my own cred. You can only hack so far. At a certain point, people have eyes and if you don't look the part, you're out.

Trust me. I've tried. All kinds of codes to get through the Gate.

No go.

"Okay. Say I did say yes. Look at me." I risk honesty. "You got a plan for this?"

RF looks me right in my metallic eyes, pointedly *not* looking me up and down like a leering creep.

I appreciate the sentiment, but not what RF says next.

"Don't exactly need a plan. You look nice."

Nice.

With my outrageously roughed-up hair, busted inlines under one arm, a shredded multi-patched skater's jacket, ugly scars adorning my dirty street-use-only body pads, a huge hole in the left shoulder of my never-been-washed shirt. Spray paint speckled across my forearms and wrists.

Nice?

"Come on, corn cob. You can't mean that," I say, blunt.

"I do, but I can see why you don't trust me."

"Trust isn't the issue, asspass," I say, rolling my eyes. "There are other humans."

RF pats something on their chest. "Taken care of. I have multi-passes."

The mythological all-access pass that gives someone the ability to bring any kind of visitors anywhere they like. Those passes aren't even supposed to exist, let alone be wandering around on a necklace around the neck of someone fairly low-grade and low-key like RF.

Unless RF really is a murdering jackhole who works for The Man and picks off par-humans in their off hours for fun.

"Can I see?" I ask, putting on a whimsical voice. Like I'm oohed and aahhhed. Humans like that kind of shit.

RF shrugs, noncommittal. "Sure, why not."

They put two small purple and blue diamond-shaped multi-passes in my hand. I get a closer look, eye nodes soaking up all the details. Funny thing is, these look almost…handmade. Like fakes without being fakes. The barcodes are totally legit, but the edges of the printing are a little ragged. And the plastic is flimsy, too flexible for what it should be.

I'd recognize shoddy work like this anywhere. It's the same kind of things skaters do when they need to get into a coded locker room. You hunt down what the pass ought to look like, find some cheezeball plastic trash lying around, melt it down with a Bunsen burner, and fashion the goo into your own little device.

Nobody ever looks too close at these. Only ever machine eyes. So if the code works, it's good. Personally, I've never been able to manage the angles of passes myself, but granJan used to make them all the time.

The fake multi-pass certainly doesn't make RF seem less like a potentially murdering jackhole. But it certainly does make them look less like a Copper Stomp. More edgy, less gov.

My intrigue short-circuits my need to run the other way. I'm going to say yes. And I'm going to finally see Hacker Haven with my own eyes. Going to step foot on the Inside.

Sure, I'm going to do it with a maybe-murderer. But if I've learned anything from adi-V-scan culture, it's this: one has to take the offers that arise in life. And if I learned one thing from being a hacker, it's: information is core.

So either way, I can't say no.

"Okay, you got me."

RF turns that hot red color humans do when they are either too shy to admit what they want, ashamed of something, or both. The mask of RF's face becomes so blood-flooded that I can see subtle patchy lines on each cheek I didn't notice before. Freckles or scars, I can't tell.

"I don't think you'll be unhappy with that decision."

"Why?" I ask, curious.

"I don't think we're so different, you and I," RF says.

I scoff. Yes, we are.

RF leans in, lowers their voice. "I mean, I think we have similar goals."

Not exactly the typical human judgey rude 'tude toward poor par-people. More like a fellow hacker. Or a Copper Stomp pretending to be a hacker.

"You have no idea what my life is like, Fleshie," I say because it's true either way.

"You're right, I don't know exactly. But I have some ideas."

"Oh please," I say, rolling my eyes.

What a *human* reply. Next this asspass is gonna say if I work hard enough, I can buy a house on the Inside. Complete junk, that line. The Gate makes it impossible. The only par-humans who ever get through do so as servants for the rich. But that line is so common it's almost a proverb. A thing humans keep repeating to make themselves feel better about the segregation their kind created.

"Not like that," RF says defensively. "I know a friend of yours."

Another classic tripe line. "I know lots of par-humans who—" fill in the duxing blank.

The thing RF doesn't know is that I don't have any friends left. After granJan disappeared, my team fell apart. We can't look each other in the eye anymore, so we stopped trying three years ago. I've been rolling solo since.

"I'm over you right now," I say deadpan, just totally over it.

"I'm sorry. I just—thought you'd want to know. That…" RF stops short. They swallow and look away. "It's nothing. I'm sorry. Got carried away. I'm being a major asspass. Forgive me."

I eye RF carefully, studying their face. They have the paling skin tone a human gets when they've just dodged a scary moment. Almost let something dangerous slip out, but caught it in time.

The butterfly war in my belly just had a new battalion added to the field. A massive surge of hope that maybe, stupidly, this asspass knows something about granJan, about that accent, about what happened three years ago. Even a hint would be worth taking a risk.

Were our places swapped, granJan would risk it for me without a second thought.

"A friend of mine?" I ask, pressing the issue.

RF gives me a sideways look, narrowed eyes, the slightest shake of their head. Their pursed lips read: "I can't say right now."

It can't be granJan. But at the same time, it has to be vem. Who else could it be?

Which proves one of two things. One: RF is granJan's killer, or two: RF is a radical human and knows where granJan is and why vey disappeared three years ago.

The risk just got thicker, richer, and deeper. One hundred percent impossible to turn way from.

"Fine," I say. A yes with barriers.

"You mean you'll come with me?" RF asks to clarify.

Do you need a contract signed in my copper-speckled semi-blood? I want to say, but don't. Rule one of staying alive: never call a murderer out before forming an escape plan. And not a cheeze one that's sure to get you killed more epically than before. A real, solid actually-saves-your-life escape plan.

"Yes, I want in, but I'm not into you—is what I'm saying," I say instead.

RF's face does a funny thing. A combination of the corners of their lips falling and their eyes narrowing, like someone who's just been told they didn't pass a test. Or won't be getting into their friend's band's concert. It's not disappointment, per say, because it's much too personal. The ache of having one's unfounded hopes dashed.

They look away quickly, as not seeing their face will make me forget what I just read in their microexpressions. Classic human error. Out-of-sight, out-of-mind isn't true for the silicone mind.

From their reaction, I'd guess they care what I think of them. Genuinely. Which is way more than I could say of any human I've ever met prior. Most brush par-humans off like dust on a surface. Insignificant, irritating. But RF seems troubled that I'm being stand-offish.

Which makes me like them more than I did a moment ago. Less in a gushy crushy way. More in a strong but soft way. Companionable. Someone who could maybe help me change the world through more than just a couple cheezeball hacks here and there.

That's what I want to do. Fix things. Fluxx Fluid over the whole city. I want to level the playing field between carbon and silicone. Help humans and par-humans see that we don't need to be enemies just because we're different.

"Shall we go?" RF asks with those too-open vowels that sounds just like granJan.

What are the chances a murderer would have picked up on a subtly like that?

What are the chances someone who *isn't* a murderer goes by a name like Razor Fade?

What the dux am I doing?

Leaning in.

"Yep."

"Let's cruise," RF says.

Cruise?

I'm about to point out the obvious fact that my inlines are way beyond help, but then RF pulls out a fold-away board from a small gray pouch that I've completely missed hanging at their side. The board, big enough for two, slaps down against the concrete, and RF gets aboard effortlessly, then reaches a hand toward me.

"Coming?" they grin, toothy and wildly human.

I like that.

I like that *too much*.

A shot of excitement goes right through my spine. Shivers like I've never felt before burst on my skin as our hands touch. Absolutely electric. Total EMP level wowza.

I climb aboard, and we kick off together, side by side. As we cruise, we manage to keep perfect balance, like we were built to roll together. We pick up speed on a long downhill, and we're tracking with traffic like I do solo. My whole chest swells. Wind whips through my hair, sending little lashes against the back of my neck. Saline leaks from the corners of my eyes.

Everything feels alive.

RF gives me the side-eye and slowly guides us off the curb. In one fluid move, we've taken the middle of the road. Beside me, RF's wide-mouth laughter fills me to the brim.

I can't help but laugh out loud because this is the most amazing and absurd thing I've ever done.

We ride like that, kick for kick, practically breath for breath until we're alongside the Wall. The Gate, huge and metallic, rises up to our right. RF kicks off first, and I follow in the hic of a breath. Like we're connected telekinetically. Uplinked to one

another's actions. Which isn't possible with a blood-and-bones, but right now, I sure wish it was. Just to get into RF's mind. Something about that feels sensual and exotic, the taste of a drink I've never heard of. I can't stop the blush creeping to my all-too-human cheeks.

"We're nearly there," RF says, graciously not pointing and laughing at me.

"Let's walk the rest of the way," I say, finishing RF's sentence without meaning to.

RF laughs instead of getting irritated by my natural conversation processor speed.

Another warm rise inside of me. "Companionable" is the right word.

Too right.

What was that about not falling for a flesh-and-blood?

RF strides ahead, right toward the heavily guarded Gate Pavilion a little too confident, and suddenly, an alarm goes off inside of me.

This is all too easy, too convenient, too nice—isn't it?

The warmth of excitement gets stabbed through with a bolt of heavy fear. I'm being groomed. Set up to fall for this charismatic jackhole. They probably have some massive file on me, data gathered over a span of years like creepers do. And all this attention and matching pairs junk is RF's way of getting me to let my guard down.

And it's working.

Oh shizzle fizzle. What am I getting myself into?

I'm taking what the universe is giving me, that's what. If RF is granJan's killer, I have to know. Whether I can fix it or not.

We come up alongside the Wall before we come to the Gate. From this close up, it looks like a long black slash across my vision. The very symbol of all I can't change in this City. All my useless attempts, my beating my body against solid tech-perfected synth-stone harder than diamonds and kevlar put together.

I stare out across the land at the shadows the Wall casts. RF notices and follows my gaze.

"Ugly, isn't it?" they ask.

I nod.

The Gate Pavilion comes into sight. A big round flatland surrounded by kevlar-clad Copper Pops armed with not-so non-lethal guns. I shiver at the sight and slow my pace.

RF reaches back, holding their hand out to me. I take it without thinking. A silent agreement that we're in this together. We cross the massive yard of concrete hand in hand. The shadows of the Copper Pops cast narrow dark lines across both our faces like war paint. I feel both brave and exposed.

We come up to a bright yellow line that cuts between the edge of the concrete Pavilion and the actual Gate. A guard in front of the passageway eyes me.

"Hey. You got a pass, metal-head?"

I open my mouth to reply and nearly choke on the knot that forms in my throat.

Did I honestly think getting through the Gate would be easy peasy one-two-threesie?

Oh, pleasie.

"Right here, with me," RF says and waves the multi-passes so fast the images are blurred.

The guard nods and ushers us forward. "Keep moving."

I squeeze RF's hand, signaling thank you. RF squeezes back, takes the first step across the yellow line of no return. I follow suit. On the other side of the line, the concrete turns to smooth fabricated marble. A high white archway rises above our heads, greeting us with a light show. Red and purple and pink, full of dancing hearts for the coming holiday. Fake drone-like silver-and-gold butterflies flit and flutter like confetti in front of us. I smile to push aside the fear of being auto-scanned, recorded, uploaded to the human-only netfeeds and turned into a living meme.

RF swats at the flies clearing a path for us and tugs me on.

We near the second archway, black faux granite, full of white specks that look like stars. I gaze up and tighten my gut. Once we're on the other side of this black archway, I won't have the chance to back out.

That's good. I owe it to granJan. I owe it to all the par-humans.

Chances like this come once in a lifetime. I'm not saying no.

RF stops at the last barrier, a thick black slash between us and the Gate's opening where the turnstiles await. On the other side, the road we're standing on will lead straight through the heart of the

Inside. It rambles through small parks and bisects big green-ways, weaves through quaint streets lined by massive single-person residences on both sides.

The only thing separating us from the Inside now is a single bar of movable metal and two huge black doors.

RF pings the multi-passes against the turnstile's access panel. A light flashes gold in our faces, the small bar slides inward and before us, the Gate swings silently open on well-oiled hinges.

I'm about to bust through the Gate as fast as I can, just get it over with, but RF gives my hand a slight tug, slowing me up. We share a look. Mine, indignant. RF's, full of warning. Their brown eyes flick up to an almost-hidden camera drone that's got its eye on us. I simmer down and take it casual slow. We stroll through together, joined arm in arm.

As we come out the other side, RF lets me go, and I feel something sink in my gut. A deep ping of disappointment I want to pretend isn't there. Why should I care if we aren't touching now?

"Let me tell you a secret," RF says after we've made it a few hundred meters away from the Gate.

I stop, heart sinking, fully expecting the secret to be a bludgeon to the head. Or a stunner stabbing through one of my protective pads. Or a flash of viral light that my silicone mind can't avoid the damage from.

I don't say anything. Just stand there waiting on mute.

"I'm not what I seem," RF says with a sigh.

Like they can read micro-expressions as well as par-human can. Like they know I think they're dangerous. They know I'm afraid for my life. They know I don't buy this whole nicey-dice act.

But they can't possibly know any of that.

I'm total pro at hiding my feelings. According to the Governmental Treatise of Humanitarian Beings: as a par-human, I barely have any as it stands. "Strictly rudimentary." Emotions that connect to the base of my semi-silicone spine. Survival instincts and the like. But nothing of depth or import. Nothing that would require a micro-expression.

Surprising how easy it is to hide something nobody is looking for.

"What do you think I am?" RF asks when I don't say anything.

I look them directly in the eyes to read what they mean. Instead of clarity, our eyes meet with sparks. Something so familiar and comfortable. Safe. Like coming home after a night spent lost in a freezing winter storm.

My belly butterflies scramble.

RF's glittery human eyes, dark brown and sparkling with the Gate's overhead lights, say I'm safe here.

I can't help but melt.

And for a second, all my worry that RF is a crazy par-human murderer melts away. RF's smile is magnetic, glowing like the morning sun at me. I can't help but smile back.

"I think you're a ridiculous, flesh-and-blood," I say, laughing.

RF doesn't say any more but takes us off the main drag as quick as possible. We walk instead of cruise now, twisting on foot down smaller and smaller side streets.

Truth is, I want it to be true. I want RF to be on my side. On the side of zero-oppression. On the side of fixing this place, making things equal for all. Tearing down the Wall. Letting the Gate stand as a reminder of our ugly past.

I want RF to not be granJan's killer, but truly my friend.

Or more. My partner in making things good again.

I want granJan to still be alive and for RF to be both my way back to an old friend and my road to a whole new life. One where the three of us could make the City whole. Human and par-human together, hand in semi-synthetic hand.

What a V-Day present that would be, eh?

Wishful thinking. The pre-V-Day ravings of a heart-broken fool.

We turn a sharp bend and come out onto a street populated with food carts and standing bars.

"Restaurant Alley," RF announces.

The street is just wide enough for two people to pass. The ground's not the usual poured concrete, but an uneven walk made of huge flat gray stones. Rows of tiny but beautiful food carts stand open, boasting real wood-bar counters and high gloss bar stools. Wood shingle roofs all slant in the same direction, creating a fancy stair-step effect. A-frame signs stand beside each window with decorative handwriting in chalk and paint that boasts each

cart's limited menu. Globe-shaped bulbs hang from one rooftop to the next.

Each cart has a single open window that pours rich buttery light onto the faces of patrons and the shoulders of passers-by. Small plates are passed from human chefs to hungry guests, and each plate towers with fresh-cut vegetables, creamy sauces, crusty fresh-baked bread. The smell is intoxicating, sweet and yeasty, savory and green. The hushed murmur that hangs over the crowd purrs with satisfaction, fulfillment, dreams coming true.

My mind rebels at that, hating each new puffed-up patron a little bit more, while my stomach grumbles and churns for more. RF keeps us moving with a light touch on my elbow. We move silent and fluid, like shadows slipping down flagstone steps. We swoop around corners of brick buildings and pass unseen under archways made of real granite and true marble.

We turn another corner and there it is.

An ornate sign announces itself in swirling silver and blue.

Hacker Haven.

It's every bit as jaw-dropping as the rumors claim. The quaint frontage is all wood counters, high gloss tables, antiquated bar stools. The whole building is decorated with actual living vines growing up posts and growing in woven natural-fiber baskets. Fruits and vegetables sit in carved stone and wood bowls on high tables. The sweet malty richness of fermented grains mixes with the sweet of caramelized sugar and floats like perfume on the air.

In the back kitchen, seen through a wide panel of glass, steam rises from massive pots the likes of which I have never seen before. There's a melancholy acoustic guitar track playing overhead.

A sign hangs nondescript and hard to notice, off to the side of the front counter space. In small ornate powder blue font, it reads: "Safe haven. All are welcome."

A real haven. It can't be, not here inside the Wall. Not on Restaurant Row. But here it is nonetheless. I shiver from a confusing mixture of excitement and dread.

RF ushers me forward toward the doorway that stands perpetually open.

Beside the counter, an A-frame sign contains words I'm certain aren't in our common language.

Letters I've never seen stuck together. "Borschtata" and "Stradets" and "perrogini" for starts. "Covfefe," the coo-de-ta swan song. I can't even begin to make sense of it.

Counter-intuitive to all this natural earthy hand-made biz, the actual counter is composite fiber and sports a super low-grade computer screen that looks mashed together from spare bits nobody wanted about a hundred years ago. The screen has chunky block font and lists a number of canned statements.

"Welcome! For Here or To Go? Extra mayo? Side of slaw? Large covfefe or small? Soda bath or chew stix? Will that be insta.Pay™ or Cash.back(R)? Voice activated or manual mode?"

Each one is a button you can select for some god-forsaken reason.

RF elbows in and hits a button I hadn't seen at first. "Start Your Order." From a drop-down menu on the far left of the screen. Right underneath a dull gray power-off/on button.

I glare up at RF, annoyed that I have to rely on a human to do a machine's job.

"Is this place a joke?" I ask, not hiding my annoyance.

RF laughs like this is the biggest joke in the world.

"Yep, okay. Thanks," I say, assuming the answer is "yes, this place is a spoof and I'm punking you. Ready to die quietly?"

This place is probably a front for the edgy Copper Stomp flavor of murdering jackhole humans who like to play with their kill, baffle and distract an otherwise completely capable par-human victim so ver not looking when the jackhole goes in for the attack.

I'm not going to fall for it.

I give RF the eagle-eye with auto-record activated. That way, when the Big Dog carnage hunters find my body, at least someone will be the wiser. Not that the Big Dogs or The Man or the richie oligarch fucks will care. But just that someone will have the information in the mainframe City database in case some par-human hacker who's the wiser ever wants to look for it.

RF gives me a sidelong glance, meeting me eagle-eye.

I stare back unblinking. Par-humans don't need to blink. We do to make humans hate us less. Right now, I couldn't care less how RF feels.

"I'm not playing you," RF defends after we've had a good minute-long staring contest.

"Of course you aren't," I say non-committal, trying to hide how scared I am at the moment.

See what I get for finding a human interesting, attractive, compelling? Neck deep in a murder plot. Dux me.

I need a plan.

I start mashing buttons, hoping to at least attraction the attention of some of the less suspecting patrons of Hacker Haven. When nobody reacts, I figure they're all in on the plot—paying bystanders who get their kicks by watching par-humans get taken for a ride then dismantled in the back. I mash buttons more frantically because I'm at a total loss of what to do next. I feel all my resolve fraying at the ends like a wire going bad, about to disconnect.

"Whoa whoa whoa," RF calls out, not to my surprise. "Cool your jets."

I don't stop.

RF gives me a nasty glare and snatches my hand.

I shake free and step back.

"You're making a scene," RF says plainly.

I turn and everyone in the place is staring at us. Eyes ogling out of their heads.

"Oh dux this place, and dux you!" I hiss, at the end of my nerve.

I turn and charge out of the death trap that is Hacker Haven. I have no idea where I'm going. I just have to get out.

"Hey!" RF shouts after me. "Wait!"

I don't stop or slow my pace. Flesh-and-blood don't really stand a chance against us when face-to-face. Hence the Wall and all their hardcore segregation efforts. They know par-humans are stronger and more fit, better and faster and more adept. They also know our intelligence outpaces them by infinity times itself. So like rabbits who've been foxed out, they burrow in deeper and huddle in closer.

Soon, they'll be no more. But the process of death is slow and tedious.

And yet. RF does catch up with me, reaches out and I feel their fleshy hand clamp around my shoulder. The touch, again, is gentler than I anticipate. Especially at this juncture.

"How did you—" I start, but RF waves the question away.

I look down and see they've gotten on their fold-a-board. Of course. That's why they have one. To catch up to victims like me.

"There's someone I wanted to introduce you to," RF says suddenly, letting my shoulder go easily. "If you recall. I said I knew a friend of yours."

I stare, confused how that matters right now.

"Trust me," RF says, as if trust is on the table.

It's not. And I don't.

I move away without a word, looking for the most obnoxious escape route so I can lose RF fast. I'll figure out getting back through the Gate when I cross that road.

Right as I slip free, the back door of the cart opens.

Perfect. Looks like running is a no-go after all. If I had my inlines, I could make a go of escape, but they're junk under my arm right now. Trash in the bin when I get home. What a shizzle fizzle fool I was to let myself get on that board with RF back on the Outside. Now, on the Inside, I get the pleasure of facing RF's whole murdering jackhole posse.

Per-duxing-fect.

I brace myself for whatever comes through that open door. It's a huge red-blooded human in tall rubber grease-slicked boots. Face sharp and angular more like a par-human, chiseled chin, steep cheeks. Eyes glint in the kitchen lights like they've had significant implants. Arms like sausages, almost the same radius as my own.

If I were to draw an image, I'd say this fleshy was a skater at one point. Maybe a few years ago, based on the ample spare weight around their middle.

The bulky human clop-trops over to me, leans down, and gives me the stink-eye. I sneer back and assume my best street-fighter's stance. And, at the same time, I prep codes to read the human's muscle motions and weight shifts. For the first two swings, I don't even need it.

I duck a sloppy attempted crack to my nose. With humans, it's always the same. They're so predictable its almost funny. Hit the nose like an off button. When the nose blow fails, they go for a wide left hook. I've been in enough post-tourny fights to know that much.

Sure enough. The human goes for shot number two.

I duck, and the human's massive arm whiffs through air.

I stand and scan the codes for this jackhole's next move.

The codes read stillness, settling, no further action. What? I stare at the cook, confused.

The cook frowns back at me, deep lines set in a wrinkle-ridden face. The frown is so stiff-lipped and low-brow that it's downright impressive. I almost applaud.

The cook opens their mouth and beyond the whiskers is a mouth full of cheap alloy-capped rot that I smell like a blast of hot sick to the face. I try not to choke, fail, and gag on the air in my mouth.

"This the one?" Fresh Breath asks. "Trying to run?"

I try to respond but my eyes are watering from the rank sewage potpourri.

RF is suddenly beside me, nodding profusely.

"This is the one," they say gently, like they're trying to save this encounter from turning into a rapid-fire fight fest typical between humans and par-humans whenever a par-human just so happens to find vemself in some nicer part of town. Regardless of circumstance or chaperone.

I glare at RF with a look of betrayal.

"This is my friend I thought you'd like," RF says gently. Not at all like the cook is murdering jackhole number two.

Friend to RF, yes. Friend of mine? I doubt that.

Luckily, I have proof on my side. I insta-replay our little fight for all to see. Only, in the playback, I see the cook trying to calm me down, not punch me out. Trying to get a hold of me, not give me the left jab. Their expression is one of concern, not hate. And I look like a short-circuiting fool flailing around with wires loose.

Shizzle fizzle. Have I just made a wreck of my chance at Hacker Haven for no reason? Are RF and Fresh Breath cook here really trying to help?

I frown at myself, a tiny micro-flinch of internal disappointment. Why do I keep doing that? Trying to see what's ace about these blood and bones asspasses? Trying to make space for RF to be kind and gentle, the kind of person I'd be willing to be companionable with.

Stupid.

It's not like RF would do the same back.

But then I look at RF and they're looking back at me with a micro-expression that's at once grateful and sad. Empathetic. Like they know what I'm feeling.

But that's impossible. Humans don't get par-human feelings. They think we're all a bunch of heartless automatons who go around loving nothing but the wires inside ourselves. All the V-Day adi-V-scans make it plain. Humans love each other, par-humans just want stuff.

But even RF's macro-expression is complicated. A half smile that turns down at the left corner of their face. The dominant side of their face, meaning trace disappointment. Those high-arced, ever-surprised eyebrows curve and fall in a way that unavoidably looks like they're hoping I can see something that's incredibly hard to see.

That they like me.

No, that's wrong.

That we're companionable.

Even worse. I can feel my wires sizzling at the mere thought. I look away quick and try to pretend I've been paying attention to the cook this whole time.

The cook's expression is blank, eyes in neutral position, eyebrows disengaged. Annoyance, but nothing dangerous. Clearly reading my face with chagrin, I think, like a par-human would. "Welp, this is fun. You two flirting and all."

Both RF and I fidget, making it clear that the cook is right.

Well dux. What do I do with that? I'm flirting with someone who's about to murder me? Have I short-circuited or what?

"Who are you?" I ask as a distraction rather than think about the answer to that question.

"Name is Janitor," RF answers importantly.

"Not exactly what I meant," I say, not caring about the asspass cook's name. What I meant was which gang. It's the least they could do, give me the honor of naming their crackpot gang, jackholes.

"Can I tell vem what happened to granJan now?" Janitor asks RF, completely ignoring me.

All the wires inside me sizzle white hot while the human parts go cold. Silly infatuation is all burned up, the rest of me frozen solid. I can't move, can't think, can't breathe. A raging between the hot and cold sweats break out across my whole body. I shiver and sneeze violently at the same time. Signs of system overload.

Chess Matey, or whatever it is humans say when they win at logic games.

RF looks down at me, about to say some really gruesome messed-up stuff. I look away because I can't meet those beautiful eyes and listen to shit like that. Not with all the ridiculous fluttery things I've felt since we met. All that attraction and pent-up hope in…what even?

Hope in the fact that a flesh-and-blood might be something different than just another richie take-over-the-city asshole who'd want to put par-humans in the ground. Hope that, if there was such a human, we'd meet and figure out a way to fix this city together. Hope that others would get on board. And we'd form a whole alliance. And finally, we'd have a way to fight back. Not gasbombs in portos. Not nicks in the Wall when someone throws broken glass. Not fires burning out hovels where someone heard a richie went once. No. A real, systemic root-change kind of chance.

But here we are.

RF is giving me that look—the one that means I'm about to get chopped up and stuck into jars. One shelf for human bits, one shelf for so-called "non-living" (my silicone parts, brain contents not excluding). And my hope in the future turns out to be one big extended nightmare that smacks of foolishness inspired by infatuation chemicals inside the fleshy parts of my brain.

If I'd used logic, I'd have known better. If I'd tapped into all my silicone-based super-intelligence, I'd have instantly seen the flaws in my thoughts. If I'd have stopped ogling RF's eye color and kept reading micro-expressions, I'd have gotten out of this before it came to my death.

But no. Those eyes just tripped right past logic into what I wanted to call love. Knew better, but wanted it anyway. Like we lifeforms do from time to time. Defeat ourselves with chasing the wrong thing.

How naïve and human of me.

To think someone with RF's status would want to tear apart the system that gives them everything they love. Har har.

"I didn't want to get your hopes up," RF says, perfectly on cue.

I keep looking at my feet. It's a pretty bizarre asshole thing to say before you kill someone, but whatever.

"It's just that the granJan you knew is gone."

"I know, asspass," I blurt out, sick of all this bullshit movie-style monologuing about how exactly these blood bags killed granJan and are now gonna kill me. For the greater good or some shit, I bet they'll say next.

"The experiments ruined ver body."

Tch, what a sick twist-tie RF is.

"But we were able to upload granJan's consciousness into a new interface."

Hold the scan. What the actual ducking dux is going on?!

I replay the words in my head on super-fast.

The truth clicks and sticks.

RF hasn't only killed granJan, but uploaded their consciousness to do some really duxed up shit. I have an imagination. I try not to use it.

I'm disgusted with myself for falling for RF, but I shouldn't be surprised. Humans can never see a par-human's humanity. Why I thought this asspass was any different is beyond me.

A trick of the eye, that's all it was. Maybe even an optical viral hack to earn my trust.

But I'm over it now. I turn on RF like the enemy they are.

"Okay, psycho. You've got my attention," I hiss, shooting my meanest look into RF's face like a laser attack. I hope it burns a hole through their face. It doesn't, and RF just keeps looking at me like I'm going to go ballistic. Which I might. But before I lose my gaskets, I add, "What do you want? Me to bow down and lick your ugly shoes?"

They aren't ugly, the shoes. But I'm not giving RF the satisfaction of knowing I think that.

RF legit gapes, stops talking, swallows hard and backs a good three steps away from me.

"Oh! Shizzle. Vey think we're murderers, Raze!" Janitor blurts in a stanky way.

Their muddy basic brown eyes so so wide I can see the hints of gold on the outer rim. Which makes me think…rip-off synthetic implants? But what is a rich blood-and-bones doing with cheap implants like those? Discs that thick would have to be junk-yard rabble. The kinds of contaminated, short-term shivs reserved for only the lowest grade of androids. The kind who don't have pain receptors because lenses like that grind against the eyelid, they're so ill-fitted and rough-hewn.

RF blinks, then the thought registers somewhere in deep processing and the look on their face goes click! Eyes wide, eyebrows two degrees beyond surprised into shocked.

"Oh dux! Did you think I've been luring you here to kill you this whole time?"

I nod because I can't see a point lying or trying to fake it at this stage. Either this is the weirdest way to go about torturing someone or these humans are for reals. Whatever the case, I'm getting tired of waiting. I want to know what happened to granJan. They know. And I want them to tell me, ASAP.

"Oh duxing shizzle! I wasn't thinking!" RF continues to blather on instead. "I mean. Shuh! Of course you'd think we're murderers. No. No way. Trust me, we aren't what you think. Not at all."

"What are you then, members of some epic skate team?" I bite back, not buying any of it.

"Not exactly," Janitor says, whose face turns a color I'm not exactly familiar with. Deep, almost-purple crimson. The color of too much blood. Like their face is a red balloon about to pop. The look is so human it makes me sick to my stomach.

"You should sit down," RF says.

"I'll do as I please." I cross my arms. If these cracks are going to kill me, they can do it with me standing up.

"Suit yourself," RF says, then pulls out a hand-held device I don't recognize.

Meanwhile, Janitor takes RF's advice and sits on the ground instead of a stool. I look back and forth from the stool to Janitor, confused as to why. I smell it before I see it. A growing pool of dark yellow liquid oozing out from between Janitor's legs. The red balloon color of Janitor's face grows deeper, more purple, veins popping up under the thin film of blotchy brown skin.

Janitor has just peed themself and made a complete mess of the cart.

So much for Hacker Haven being a place of beauty, quality, and prestige.

Pee sauce anyone? Pee sausage? Pee soup?

Ew.

What kind of sick twisted murderer of par-humans pees themselves at the mention of a prior victim's name?

RF gives me a look that's at once apologetic and defensive. Eyes narrowed, lips pursed, brow furrowed in concern (for Janitor? For Hacker Haven's rep? For me?). The look, I can't help but think, is gentle and sweet.

A flicker of rage flares up into a bonfire inside my chest.

"What the dux is wrong with you all?" I scream in frustration. Not just at RF and Janitor; at all of humanity.

"New body, new rules," RF says, like that's an explanation.

I don't respond because I can't figure out how to.

"You never knew granJan's real name, did you?" RF asks.

"Like it matters," I spit, angry that RF here thinks they know more about granJan than I do.

"I think it does," RF snaps back, putting on that same rage-making sweet face.

I want to rip it off, kick off the curb, and get the dux out of this confusion vortex. Is everything inside the Wall this wacked out?

I get it now. They're having a good laugh at my expense. This is part of the torture. A mental game to make me fritz out. It's working, regardless of how idiotic their claims are, and that makes me angrier. I lose it and throw a punch.

It connects square to RF's jaw, who didn't even try to duck or block.

Take that!

Janitor comes toward me, and I swing again. Only this time, I don't just miss. I'm taken by the forearm and swung down on the ground. Flat on my back, sprawled out before the stairs of Hacker Haven's back door, urine dripping on my forehead.

Should have seen that coming. It's a pretty classic skate trick. Refs use it to break up fights on the rink. granJan was just about the only skater ever bold enough to adapt it for in-rink use on other opponents. It became a classic move the refs couldn't exactly call a foul and no skater could avoid.

And that's when it hits me.

That toss isn't your run-of-the-mill ref toss. It's granJan's signature move.

And it's not urine dripping onto my forehead. It's Fluxx Fluid!

The typically pale-yellow suspension can turn a dark amber when it's having to encourage silicone-based sections of a newly-issued par-human body to cooperate with all the organic carbon-based sections. In that state, the fluid takes on the function of spinal fluid mixed with liquid bone marrow. Full of artificial stem cells and stuff. It fights rejection and infection, hard core. Toward the end of the process, as the body starts working on its own, the mixture can smell way more rank than usual Fluxx Fluid does. Hence why I didn't immediately recognize it.

Usually, it takes about three full years for a new par-human casing to become autonomous and dump its first batch of rancid Fluxx Fluid mix.

I get to my feet, my face feeling like a bloated red balloon for the first time in my whole life.

"granJan?" I stammer in shock.

"Janitor," says granJan in that tone of voice that's both respectfully gentle and firmly correct.

"J-janitor," I say, correcting myself to use granJan's real name. "How did you—how are you—what's going on?" I finally settle on the most basic of questions.

"Let's get you both cleaned up first," RF says, gently reminding both of us that we're dripping in internal fluids.

RF goes around the back of the cart where there's another door I hadn't seen before. A few taps on a small screen and a door opens to reveal a narrow concrete flight of stairs. Janitor goes first, then me, and RF brings up the rear, closing the door behind us. The stairwell is lit dimly so I have to tread with care.

The door at the bottom is matte concrete with a single chunky padlock. Janitor puts in a series of easy-to-recall numbers (Fibonacci sequence starting with pi) and the lock pops off. Inside, there's a room that looks exactly like granJan's skater stall, complete with a poster of the full team and a 3-D projection of the trophy we won in our last skate tourny together.

I tear up at the sight of all that memorabilia. Janitor rubs my shoulder in a familiar way, small circles near the jacked-up circuitry in my left shoulder I got from a bad fall about a dozen seasons ago. The touch is warm and safe, and I melt into the comfort of it.

"You still skate?" Janitor asks.

I frown, holding up my broken inline. "Would."

Janitor nods and sighs in a way only granJan would sigh. Fritzy and digitized, a total par-human remix of human sorrow.

"I can't believe you're alive, after all this time," I say breathless.

"I can't believe Razor actually managed to find you," Janitor says back. "You weren't easy to track down."

"That's exactly what I'm going for." I smile.

RF comes into the room with a look of disgust that reminds both of us that we're supposed to be getting cleaned up. Looking for a bathroom door, I accidentally catch RF's eyes, studying me. It's not a bad look, that micro-expression, but it is hard to read. Awe? Intrigue?

Admiration. Like I'm something special.

My whole body goes on the fritz, and my cheeks burn red all over again.

"Ahem, so you have a shower and a change of clothes, or what?" I ask clumsily tripping on my words.

"There." Janitor points at the poster.

I peel it back to find a cramped little shower with just enough space for one person (par-human or otherwise) to turn around. I gingerly set my inlines down against the wall, peel off my clothes and get under the steamy stream of water. Janitor's dumped Fluxx Fluid flows off my naked body, slick and smooth like hands touching me everywhere. And it's all I can do to stop thinking of RF, of those living earth-colored hands, all pores and tiny hairs sliding along my body. Smiling lips kissing mine. Warm brown eyes soaking me in with that expression.

Admiration.

It's not sex I want.

I don't have the gear, but even if I did—I don't have the brain chemistry for it. Nothing in me yearns to know what sex feels like. Like those without optic nerves can't long to know sight. There is nothing inside of me that longs to fuck.

No.

What I want is something deeply physical. An all-sensory experience. Getting lost, adrift in the sensations of another's touch, breath, bodily warmth. Sharing synapses of wires inside our nerves, paired chemicals going off in our brains leaving us wrapped up in one another and carried off into pure bliss.

"You almost done?" RF calls.

"One minute," I say, pulling myself up out of my fantasy.

I climb out of the stall and find a pair of Janitor's clothes waiting for me. Also, my skates—all fixed. The clothes aren't quite my style, but I put them on anyway. Pinstriped blouse that hangs loose around my steep shoulders. Leggings that fit at an awkward twist. I roll out, still trying to roll up the slightly too-big waistband of soft green parachute-style over-pants. It's a look I can imagine the new curvier, well-rounded version of Janitor pulling off easily. On my straight line of a body, it just feels sloppy. But the repaired skates under my arm make everything feel just right.

I come out and Janitor chuckles at my look. RF is gracious enough to not make comment.

Janitor heads to the shower room, leaving RF and me alone on the only seat in the room: a love seat that's not big enough for us to avoid contact. I can feel the human warmth careen off their leg pressing against mine through the not-quite-thick fabric of Janitor's snazzy pants.

"So uhh…what are you two doing here?" I say to fill the awkward silence.

RF's face lights up. "Trying to start a revolution. A par-human and human collaborative effort."

"How's that going?" I ask, trying hard not to sound as skeptical as I feel.

"You can guess. Not great. Which is why we need your help, Blue Jay."

"JJ Blue," I say, giving RF my real name for the first time.

RF nods knowingly. They knew my real the whole time.

I glance at the shower where granJan—Janitor is cleaning off. I nod back. "So, why me? I mean, aside from being gran—ahem Janitor's friend from another life."

"Vey say you're an ace hacker. Someone who can get us all kinds of access."

"I've been known to," I admit bashfully. I don't like to air my accomplishments, them being illegal and all.

"I heard about the stunt you played when your team won the championship."

"Free Sausage Box for everyone with less than ten creds in their account! Ha!" I laugh at the memory.

It was pretty funny, all those starving skaters getting a bite of the richies' meat pie.

"And the time you ran that slot on the SuperMat Green Grocer's Mart CEO."

I frown. I wouldn't expect a human to like that stunt. I exposed the CEO as a fraud and par-human abusing dux-head who sold par-human kids into a labor black market to keep his prices "competitive" in Restaurant Row. The whole thing became a big deal in par-human right's debates. Sparked riots and labor strikes. A whole third of the Inside lost services for months. Eventually, the Copper Stomps attacked the protestors and had them all arrested. Needless to say, par-humans stopped striking after that.

"I was a Gate guard during those months," RF says soberly. "I saw the carnage. The whole Pavilion covered in a meter deep of dark amber Fluxx Fluid. I was cruising the Pav on my board, cleaning ooze up, when I met granJan. Vey were running from a hellbent Copper Stomp. I helped vem escape, and we went into hiding together. Been waiting for the right moment ever since."

Three years of hiding, waiting, looking for me.

Razor Fade is definitely *not* what I thought they were.

"You couldn't have been more right about me," I say at length. "And I couldn't have been more wrong about you. I'm sorry."

"It's your job not to trust humans like me," RF grins knowingly. "I should have realized you'd think I was a murdering jackhole though. Sorry about that one."

I shrug. "Sorry about lowkey hating you."

RF shrugs like that's completely normal. "I'm not exactly the first partner you'd pick. I get that."

I can hear past-me saying in bitter tones: *I'm not into you is what I'm saying*. The words burn hot in my gut.

"I like you," I blurt suddenly, then look away, abashed.

RF laughs, shocked, then regains composure quicker than any human ever. "You know, your adi-V-scans back in the day were one of a kind. Cutting edge. Legit anti-Man rhetoric. Very subtle, well hidden. You should be proud."

A mixture of anxiety and excitement blooms inside my chest. Nobody has ever personally looked into my hacking stunts. Or called me "cutting edge." Or said, "You should be proud."

RF is like my first fan ever. Which as a hacker is a weird, conflicted sensation because I've always wanted to hide my name. To disappear. To be the invisible cause of change.

"You're amazing is what I'm saying," RF says quieter, biting their lip.

Bashfulness, macro-expression. Like that was really hard to admit.

"I know my way around this City like nobody. And Janitor's passes can get us into places, sure, but that's all useless without the right codes. We need a hacker like you if we're going to succeed."

I don't color at the compliment this time because RF's line of logic makes perfect sense to me.

"So, what's our plan?"

The wall hanging swings back, and out comes Janitor in granJan's old skating gear. Only it's been altered to fit the new body. Tailored perfectly. I could swear I was looking at the old granJan right now. Different shape but the same insides.

granJan's micro-expression database has all been retained. I'd know that half-smile anywhere.

"Razor Fade and I were thinking the City could use a real ace V-Day present," Janitor says with a granJan flourish.

One arm up, at a forty-degree angle. The other down, at fifty-five. Legs in a crisscross. A stance that, in skates, would be a twirl. Flat-footed, it turns into a flowery bow. No less fitting.

My eyes narrow. "A V-Day present?"

Janitor laughs in a way that sounds strange. It's going to take some getting used to, this new version of my old friend. I believed for three years vey were certainly dead.

"A whole counter-culture adi-V-scan campaign," RF says.

Sounds stupid, I almost say. Then I catch myself. This human being a part of a City-wide reunion revolution is harder to get used to than the new granJan. This might be the only human I've ever known who's not a total jackhole full of richie shite. I don't even know what that looks like on the Inside. Shizzle, I don't even know what it looks like on the Outside, aside from "like RF."

I admit. I like the idea more than I should.

That the only good human is, in part, mine.

The fluttery butterflies are back in my belly, only this time I know they aren't fearful of being murdered or in the wrong place at the wrong time. Exactly the opposite. This feels just like being in the rink back in the team's heyday. The right place, the right time, the right people by my side. My tummy overflows with excitement and hope.

For changing the world, yes, but also for finding love.

"I like it," I say finally, accepting RF's idea, something I'd never think of.

"Thanks," RF says, and reaches for my hand, then hesitates.

I take RF's hand in mine. The flesh against my semi-synthetic is delightful. Warm with cool. Damp with dry. A perfect balance.

"We'll make a load of adi-V-scans that give people truths instead of selling them junk. We give them the gift of real information," Janitor elaborates.

"I like it," I say, already thinking of all the codes I could write, all the cheesy adi-V-scans that will be easy to pick off and replace with a handmade script. All the minds we can reach without them even knowing we're there, waiting with the truth about their world.

"Truth bytes!" RF says, squeezing my hand. "You can even make the intro-screen red and pink. Lots of hearts, if you want."

I laugh, a shot of thrilling energy going all the way up my arm to my shoulder where my old injury reminds me of past failure and pain. Janitor notices my micro-flinch and rubs my shoulder. The sensation is different from RF's touch. Calming and serene like laying down after a long day. All these sensations— excitement and fear, love and anger, yearning and ease—all co-exist inside of me. A reminder that one thing never exists without another.

Like humans and par-humans. Our little group here is just a microcosm of the truth.

Like a body, we are stronger as a whole than the mere sum of our parts. Part carbon-based, part silicone-based. All symbiotic infrastructure. The real revolution is when all of us realize we don't exist without one another.

It's time the City knew.

"Let's do it," I say, squeezing RF's hand in mine.

RF squeezes back, and my butterflies go crazy while my heart aches. I still shouldn't be falling for a human. Even if RF is part of the resistance. Even if RF is ace friends with Janitor here who is, without a doubt, my granJan. Even if RF is the reason granJan got free from the City. Even if RF found me to help start a revolution. Even if together we're going to try and fix the City.

It's not just the human/par-human stuff. It's the fact that RF and I aren't on equal footing, no matter how you swing it. I'm just some scrappy underground hacker with inline skates so busted I couldn't even roll out of here. And RF is everything else. Everything I wish I had, RF started out with. Everywhere I wish I could go, RF was born to be a part of.

Falling in love like that is just asking for a wad of trouble.

I know better.

And yet, the butterflies won't go away.

What if RF is exactly the person the revolution needs? Like my hacking skills, RF's accesses inside the Wall are something the revolution has been waiting for. Like Janitor's connections from our skate tourny days.

None of us can do it alone, but we can do it together. We *need* to do it together with our differing approaches. The three of us make one ace team, when you look at it like that.

"We'll start simple, something to get people's attention," Janitor says after we're in front of some screens.

RF, fleshy palm still pressed against mine, gives my arm a light shake. "What do you think?"

"I think we should start with the Mall the night of," I say. "Everyone will be getting last minute gifts and making last second reservation check-ins. It's the perfect setting for mass distribution."

"Think like a corp. *Go big or don't go at all*," RF laughs.

That line's a direct quote from an adi-V-scan we all know from childhood. It was for skates, flashy and rink ready, that had magnetic force fields to keep them safe. That skate adi-V-scan played before every morning cartoon. Shows just how effective the tactic is.

"Exactly," I say, cheezing wide at RF for the reminder.

RF is being super corn-doggy saying stupid adi-V-scan lines like they're common slang. It's super loser status, and that makes it endearing and cute.

"Okay, what do you need?" Janitor asks, looking at me.

"Working on it," I mutter, pulling up my access terminal, already stringing codes together, already turning the idea into ones and zeros.

V-Day, early evening.

The three of us are standing on top of the Wall where no one ever goes. Three rip-off all-access badges dangle from our hips. We can see the whole city sprawling out below us like a circuit board. I watch the steady flow of tacky heart-covered Road Rovers clearing away the snow that fell early this year. A sign of a hard winter coming. Blippy one-person autos with pink tire chains on crawl by one another while bundled up inline skaters and coat-laden boarders zip in between them carrying heart-shaped boxes and bags in red and pink.

The last minute crowd. Our waiting victims.

From up here, I can see how the City is really just one big machine. Each individual part, a free-acting node. Each avenue, a line of code. Trouble-shooting the problems of society feels less daunting from this angle. Tangible. Like I already know what patches I need to write to make the right codes flow. I can imagine the shifts in real-time, watch the City morph into something new in my mind's eye.

Like running diagnostics on a mainframe.

Our revolution is going to succeed. I know it.

Not because we're all that extra ace smart or because any one of us is the most incredibly talented at one thing or another. No. We're going to succeed because this is mathematical resistance. Use the right ones and zeros, put a string of code in the right place, and the machine will do exactly as you designed.

Oppression and freedom come in the same form. Patterns we are taught to follow. Alter the source code, and the pattern will change. Write the correct algorithms, effectively distribute them, and alter the course of history.

Life is all programming.

"Ready?" RF asks, holding out a hand-held screen toward my chest.

I take it. This device, handmade by RF in the back room of Hacker Haven, has all the codes installed on it we need to break into the adi-V-scan system.

It's not the only key to unlocking the Gate, but it is the first one. The most important.

"Ready," I say, and look at Janitor.

A silent nod.

It's time.

I hit a blue blinking [Install] button. Blue for "go."

The adi-virus uploads. A little orange bar slowly growing. I suddenly can't breathe. All those butterflies, the icy ones of fear and the warm ones of excited joy, swarm inside of me so fast I feel my stomach about to give. Fluxx Fluid about to eject like a projectile from my throat. Then, I feel flesh against my silicone.

RF's head on my shoulder. The soft tickle of their hair against my cheek. Their arm pressed against my side. As I breathe out my held breath, I can feel our chests rise and fall in perfect unison.

Just like that first time, skating together on RF's board.

There's just something about us that's perfectly timed. Two complimentary codes that worked pretty okay on their own but work far better when put together.

Out on the circuit board of the City, we can see the big screens flicker and turn a soft soothing indigo color. RF's idea. That color is mathematically the most chill color in the whole universe. Incredibly difficult to get right, but with the equation before me, it was easy to code in.

Down below, the whole churning City falls still. Just for an instant. Every eye watches the intro sequence to our viral educational series. It calls every person, human or par-human, by name. A heart-shaped banner floats across a library backdrop.

"Love Note for You" a smiling Valentine says in a childlike voice.

"Free Content" flashes before the user's view.

A short video auto-begins.

A room appears, backdropped by the massive unmistakable black and white flag of The Man. A clip-art style robotic arm crossed with a photo-realistic human arm, and in the foreground a shadow cutout of a man's bearded face dominates the space.

In front of the flag, a massive circular black marble table fills the room. Ten ancient humans sit at the table, arranged in a semi-circle. Their clothes, all identical black and white pantsuits. Their collective skin tone is so creamy, so sunless it's nearly transparent. Like fish stuck in a dark cave their whole lives. Each wears a long white beard glistening with heavily applied beard oil. These men lean blotchy hands against withered faces, run bony fingers through their thin fading gray hair. Deep-lined frowns of fear mixed with rage cover every single face.

These are the oligarchs of old. The original makers of The Man. The last undying remnant relics of the old world's ugly male-dominated past.

In the middle of the spacious room stand two life-sized models, naked so you can see all the details. One is made of deep brown porous flesh. The other is part silver-gold, part clear silicone-flesh. Human and par-human. The old men grumble, frown heavily, make expansive gestures at the naked statures.

"We can't have all these neo-humans and par-humans mixing like this!" one says in a wheezy tone.

"If they keep working together, they'll take control of the City away from us in no time," says another.

"Think of all the monetary losses we'll incur!"

"We can't stand for this!"

"We must divide them."

"We can use scientific-sounding newsbytes to convince the humans they're better than par-humans on some innate evolutionary level."

"We'll give the humans special privileges, so they believe us double-fast."

"Better houses. Better food. More space."

"We'll build a huge wall to keep them away from each other."

"We'll even pass laws that allow par-humans to live in par-standard conditions."

"We'll alter the pay rates. Any par-human makes less, starting at five percent. They'll hardly notice at first."

"We'll encourage law enforcement to go harder, be less forgiving to par-humans."

"It's perfect."

"We'll own the City in no time."

The viral feed ends.

That's not the end of the story, but keeping our edu-vids short and sweet make them digestible. Give the City time to swallow. Just like a true adi-V-scan campaign, we have an ace plan. We'll give people time to think, adjust, take the information into themselves. Then, when they think they're alone, we'll hit them with another clip. We'll interrupt them shopping for their food packets. Catch them in line at a Derby Tourny while they wait for their snacks to come up. Interject truths into their dinner conversations when someone goes to look at a drink menu. Blare them from the sides of passing mega-busses in slanty neon font.

I feel as if I've been training my whole hacker career for this moment.

I glance at RF and the expression on their face, micro and macro, is exactly the same as mine. Despite our differences in execution, it's like staring into a mirror of my heart. Excitement so thorough, so deep and so complete, that it turns into hope for a better world all on its own.

Down below, the City has started moving again. Only this time, the movement is new and strange. Par-humans and humans on both sides of the wall stopping to stare up at it for the first time maybe. The pauses create a traffic flow pattern that slowly spreads. People crossing streets they've never crossed before. Skaters take new routes that head through human parts of town, and vice versa. At an intersection, a par-human work transport auto gives leeway to a human party mega.bus. At another, a mega.bus hits its brakes to prevent slamming into a cluster of par-humans taking a little too long to cross the street.

And just like that, the revolution has begun.

I turn to face RF on my left. Our eyes meet and for a second, I feel like the par-human in the viral feed. Standing before all those ancient relics of a past we don't need to keep reliving. Something clicks. All this "I can't love a human" noise in my head has been exactly that—programming I don't need.

I lean toward RF, reaching on my tiptoes for our noses to meet like they did when we first crashed into one another.

RF leans in toward me too.

Our noses meet.

"It's happening," RF whispers, lips close to mine.

The wind slips in the very small space between us. All my butterflies turn warm, converted in this moment of closeness. This sharing.

"Happy V-Day," Janitor says to both of us.

I laugh because V-Day feels like an even bigger joke than it did before. Day One of our revolt. Our love letter to the City.

"Happy V-Day," RF says closer to me, sweeter than ever.

I smell sweetness and salt on their skin. Very human. I'm intoxicated.

"Can I kiss you?" I ask with a sudden abandon I rarely feel. Like a new code has risen up inside of me and it's breaking chains I didn't even know I had retained from being raised in a broken, segregated city.

Instead of words, RF places their lips against mine.

The taste is at once familiar and strange, sweet and savory. The salty bite of saline is like having Fluxx Fluid coursing across a broken tooth, and the velvet of RF's tongue is like sweet candy against my gums. I press myself against RF's body, soaking up the sensations all so unexpectedly delicious I never want to leave this union.

On my other side, Janitor sighs happily, like seeing RF and me together is something vey've been waiting for a long time.

I feel the same.

And I can't wait to see how, together, the three of us try to fix the City.

Because, just like the first viral scan, I know it's going to work.

People just need to know they can say "yes" to freedom and autonomy.

It's simple coding. They just need access to it.

That's what the three of us—the whole of resistance for now—are here to do.

RF and I pull away from our soft kiss at the same time, turn and look out at the City. All those circuits. All those lines, moving. And for the first time, it looks so full of hope.

My hands, one in RF's and one in Janitor's, are both warm despite the freezing cold.

Talk about a real ace V-Day present.

It's going to be one of the hardest winters on record, I know it.

But with RF and Janitor at my side, I'm ready.

Bring it on.

Copyright © 2019 by Rei Rosenquist.

Alice Faris grew up in a small community in Northern California that proudly boasts of having more cows than people. She raised guide dogs for the blind, is dyslexic, and can shoot a gun or bow and miraculously never hit the target (which at some point becomes a statistical improbability). Alice worked as a school psychologist and counselor for local schools and currently volunteers for American Red Cross on the Disaster Mental Health team. Alice also writes paranormal romance as Tina Gower. She won the Daphne du Maurier Award for Mystery and Suspense (paranormal category), and was nominated for the Romance Writers of America® Golden Heart®. She has professionally published several short stories in a variety of magazines and written several novel series which you can find by visiting www.tinagower.com or www.alicefaris.com.

LATE TO VALENTINE'S

by Alice Faris

*H*ell of a thing waiting for your soul mate, Mary Amble thought as she glanced at the clock again. And her soul mate wasn't punctual. Okay, good to know. She's spent far too long going for the organized sort. Maybe that had been her problem with true love. Too similar. Mary was organized; supposedly she needed someone who caused her disarray. Chaos. Wildness.

She shivered at that last thought. In theory the strong, brave warrior would sweep her off her feet. They'd become enveloped into a suspenseful courtship. Adventure. In reality? Mary leaned toward the reliable sort. Or maybe that was because she'd been stood up. Again.

"So sorry. I'll call one more time to see what's keeping our participant," Miles, the researcher in charge of her love connection, said.

He poked his head in for a moment, and paused as if he were about to say more, thought better of it, and instead clicked the door shut again.

Her sister had put her up to this. She'd seen a flyer at one of her college psychology classes. Find True Love, it had promised. Mary had expected a gimmick. Like the kind someone would fumble into looking for a free vacation and winding up with the doors locked and seven hours of hard sales tactics pumped at her to sign up for a timeshare she couldn't possibly afford. Okay, yes. That might have actually happened and she vowed never to be so naive again.

But this…*this* had been different. She attended the brief information meeting. Ten minutes tops. Several researchers out of Curie Tech had gotten a huge grant to study how romantic relationships are formed. Each potential candidate would be screened, background checked, and if chosen for the full study would have health insurance covered while participating, plus a small stipend for each year they continued if they got funding beyond five years for a longitudinal focus on successful couples. Mary needed the insurance, that's what brought her to the meeting, but getting a soul mate as a bonus? Sounded too good to be true. After the ten-minute run down, if candidates wanted to move forward, they signed a permission slip—or okay, not that exactly, an informed consent that everyone would need to sign, confirming they understood the nature of the study. Then background checks were scheduled, interviews, an online personality quiz (or participants could go into the lab to take the test, whatever was more convenient), but Mary wasn't a student at the college, and she'd rather answer questions about the types of men she were attracted to in private.

Too bad there hadn't been a check box for punctual. She would have checked it. Or maybe not, depending on who walked through that door and if they were her true love. She needed a date to stick to receive the insurance. After the private school she'd worked for lowered their plan, it no longer covered birth control which she needed to keep several other hormonal issues in check and keep her out of constant cramping pain. But she also wanted a good match. Someone to be her plus one. Someone to watch the newest Netflix hit with. Instead this science-tested romance wasn't any better than what she'd been doing with an app for online dating. Could be worse, she could have been stood up for dinner on a blind date for Valentine's Day. That had been how she'd gotten into this mess—so sure that this experience would be different. To think that had only been three weeks ago.

And she was still being stood up. According to science it was apparently her destiny. She pulled out her phone and scrolled through her collection of e-books. At least the heroes in her romance novels always showed up.

Hank Jones probably should have shaved before he crashed his best friend's date, but that afterthought would need to take its place in line with all his other misgivings about what he was about to do. For starters, deceive a group of researchers who might toss him out on his hide once they realized he was one of those things that was not like the other. Next, he'd also be hoodwinking some poor lady into believing he was dating material. Lastly, it was probably illegal, but not the first time he and Henry had done this little swap-a-roo.

Came in handy that his bestie had the exact same name and they used it often for times like this. Henry Jones, his friend, not himself—let's call himself Hank to keep them straight, that's what the two did—had been between jobs again and the VA is a pain to work with, so lo and behold a research study appears that offered him an out: participate in this study and get much better health insurance that would be reliable even if his work kept dropping him. And at a cost of free, it was affordable. However, Henry hadn't counted on getting the flu right before his first date. He also managed to get a job right away and only needed to wait a few weeks for that insurance to kick in. Cue best friend with the same name on his ID card to save his sneezing, coughing, stuffy-nosed ass.

In grade school they'd groaned over the multiple times teachers and administrators confused them. Hank's mom once had to pay for Henry's lunches because of a mix up. Henry's dad had been called on accident when Hank punched Tommy Jitter when Tommy called Hank's mother an obese slob. By high school they'd figured out a way to work the system. Much like twins showing up for each other's job shifts, Henry and Hank Jones swapped themselves in all sorts of situations that suited them. Lose a bet? Stand in line for your buddy at the DMV. Got a party to provide libations for, but you're not twenty-one for another few months? Get your older, wiser name twin to make the beer run and invite him to the party.

But this would be the first time Hank would date for Henry. He wondered how the researchers would react if they knew Henry had been in an off-and-on committed relationship since he'd been medically discharged from the marines. On the flip side he wondered if Kendra had been aware Henry's insurance fix included him going on multiple dates with other women? She wouldn't put up with it for long.

Best not to get involved there. He'd go on this one date and step away from that mess.

He glanced down at Henry's text. *Research Building One. Curie Tech University. Annette Miller. That's my date's name. Thanks for doing this. Be there at 2pm. You're the best.*

He frowned down at the message and replied, *I'm here now. Please tell me you'll have a steak and beer waiting for me when I get home as my gift. One of many gifts I'll require from you for this.*

The three dots danced on his screen indicating Henry had been crafting a quip, but he didn't get a chance to read it because as soon as the elevator doors opened an arm hooked him and pulled him into the hallway. "Are you here for the date? You're late!"

The panicked man in the white lab coat gestured fervently for him to follow. "Studies show first impressions are often the longest lasting and hardest to break. You can call me Dr. Miles. Miles is my first name. First names make people feel more relaxed and appear friendlier, according to a study conducted in 2014 by the Milgram Institute. Though that one has yet to be verified with the same results as the first trial."

"Uh, okay." Hank quickened his pace.

The nerdy guy had short legs compared to Hank's long muscular ones, but he was a speedy devil. "It's a dance lesson. I hope you're able to move around in those boots. Didn't you get the e-mail? Comfy tennis shoes?"

"I, um…" Hank fumbled in his shirt for his ID, assuming they'd question him. But why would they assume someone with the same name would attempt to crash a date? Also he'd been late? It was barely one-thirty and he'd thought he'd have enough time to make himself a little more presentable after hopping on a motorcycle in the rain for the short ride to the university.

"Wait here," the researcher said, and propped a door open to a room, revealing a larger room. The linoleum tiles gleamed of fresh wax. The blinds tipped at an angle to allow in the sun's rays. Even though it had been raining, that moment the clouds broke, and the light streamed in, blinding him.

Hank lifted his hand to cut the glare, moving to the side to get a better view into the room and caught the gaze of a woman. Her eyes were rimmed in defeat, but she held her chin high anyway. Black hair slicked into a bun on top her head. Black framed glasses perched on her nose and the best naughty librarian outfit…

She gave a nervous head bob as a greeting and glanced away, unable to hide the disappointment that crossed her features.

Now, that just wouldn't do. He marched toward her sticking out his hand. "Hey."

"Hey," she responded, unsure, a blush creeped up her neck to her cheeks.

The blush interested him, especially as she kept her hand firm in his. If she were naturally shy, she pushed right through it. Going by her grit alone, he suspected she didn't let people get her off her guard.

"I'm so sorry. I should have double checked the date. I was told two—"

She shook her head as if dismissing his apology. "It doesn't matter."

"It does matter."

She offered him a faint conciliatory smile—he knew the look because he got it often. This woman had judged him already as not being boyfriend material. A quick fuck, but not someone she'd spend the rest of her life with—except the unsure tilt to her head and the stolen looks she gave him had been new to him.

And for some insane reason, for the first time in Hank's life, that look of dismissal didn't give him relief but panic that he'd already disappointed the woman who—he couldn't explain why—intrigued him.

The man looked at Mary the same way she would look at a slice of pizza right about now. She'd skipped lunch, had way too light of a breakfast, and her stomach fluttered with what could only be explained as sudden onset hunger. The guy strolled in, intense stare, wet auburn hair that had been weeks past due for a cut, and stubble to match. He sported a leather jacket, deep blue, nearly black jeans, forest green shirt with a scrap metal company logo on the front—a few holes decorated the hem, alerting Mary that he hadn't spent much time getting ready for the date.

Calvin, the name came to her, that was the person she'd been scheduled to meet. Funny, he didn't look like a Calvin. She'd been expecting an accountant, not a romance cover model who made her sex drive kick on unexpectedly and her ovaries tingle.

"Do you know how to…?" Calvin raised an eyebrow and gestured to the floor where they'd soon be whipping around like Grace Kelly, or more modernly, Channing Tatum. Mary held back a giggle at the thought of her date busting a move.

"I've never taken lessons before," she answered. "But I've always wanted to."

He nodded. "Yeah. Me too." He continued to nod as if he were convincing himself of that fact.

"Really?" She pressed her lips together, the threat she'd laugh out loud heightened.

"No." He shook his head and let out a long breath. "I'm lying. I'm a bit of a klutz."

Mary openly laughed at that and then covered her mouth. "I'm sorry. That's probably not funny for you."

His face broadened into a wide grin. His teeth were showing; his eyes lit up.

Mary's stomach did that thing again where it dipped and swerved. She really should have eaten before this thing. Now she'd be dancing, expending more energy and working up an appetite.

"So, Annette…" her date said, and his gaze fell to the ID he grasped in his palms.

Why had he been holding his ID? She'd registered a second later that he'd called her the wrong name. Had he meant it as another joke? As in a Disney Mouseketeers reference? She blinked a few times, trying to read his expression that went serious as he cleared his throat.

Their dance instructor waved them over to the front of the gym, cutting off whatever he'd been about to say. Mary wasn't sure if she should pull Calvin aside and ask him what had caused him such concern. But when she attempted to engage him his expression went back to happy-excited-to-be-here again and Mary wondered if she imagined that gloomy moment.

The instructor showed them a few simple moves and they were instructed to mimic. Mary concentrated, watching her form in the mirror. She sneaked a peek at her date.

Her date had been sneaking a peek at her. They both looked away quickly.

"Now hands on your partner." The instructor guided her hands to her partner's shoulder, his to her waist and their other hands together. "Now one, two, three—"

Mary stepped forward at the same time Calvin did and they bumped into each other. Then Mary overcorrected by pulling back quickly at the same time Calvin swung to his left, and in the physics battle over who had more mass and muscles Calvin won.

Their instructor kept a patient expression plastered on her face. "All right. Let's go over the moves one more time." She placed her hands on Calvin's hips from behind. "We need you to square up, Calvin."

It took her date a moment to respond. He straightened, but his brow wrinkled and his mouth turned down with a frown.

"Now, Mary…"

Calvin frowned harder—if that were possible.

Mary followed the dance instructor's directions. Then corrected her posture as the instructor sped away to restart the music. Calvin snorted and leaned in close, whispering. "Are you ready for this, *Annette*?" He put extra emphasis on the nickname he'd given her.

His voice rumbled rich and deep. She wished he'd say her real name just to hear how it sounded on his lips. She rolled her shoulders, using it as an excuse to move closer. "As ready as you are, Calvin."

He made a funny face, then smiled. "I'm ready to be whoever you want me to be."

"It's okay. I know this is just for insurance," she said to keep things real between them, but also keeping her voice down so the researcher couldn't hear. "I'm in a similar situation. My work cut benefits to a medication I need to function. It's not life or death, but it means I'll be pain free. How about you?"

"Yeah."

"But if I find a good person to spend nights and weekends with then bonus, right? If we fall madly in love then we should at least set our expectations from the beginning," Mary said, and then regretted her joke. What if he took her seriously—

He laughed, cutting off her doubt that their senses of humor wouldn't align. "Then you should know, I think toilet paper should face out. Deal breaker if it faces in."

"No deals broken yet."

The music started again, and she steeled herself against the second try after their initial failure. This time their feet cautiously moved the steps. A little clumsy, but no risk for injuries.

"Hobbies?" he asked.

"Shooting skeet," she answered without thinking, then she corrected herself. "No." She shook her head. "I've been experimenting with baking." Her sister had said to keep the skeet habit on the downlow considering it attracted the wrong kind of guy. She didn't jive well with the rough-and-tough, shoot 'em up crowd, she matched better with someone more sophisticated who would mix well with her more liberal family. Except all those guys she'd dated were horrified to find out she was into guns. Even though she didn't shoot animals, just clay pigeons. And yeah, she was for sensible gun laws and keeping them away from people who would do harm. The guys she dated who were into her gun habits were a little too into guns and the NRA for her tastes.

"Shooting skeet?" He attempted to swivel her into a turn as the instructor suggested. They made a rocky transition but survived the move.

The instructor clapped. "Good! Keep practicing. I'm going to return this call." She waved her phone in the air as she headed for the door. Her high heels clacked on the glossy floor. No doubt the interruption was planned so the researcher could make notes how the two participants would react to each other unchaperoned.

Mary contemplated all the topics she could deploy to change the topic, but in the end decided she didn't have anything to lose if she were honest and wouldn't gain anything by lying. "My dad was in the army. He used to take us out, my sister and me, hunting. We never took to the animal killing part, hence the clay pigeons, but I've always enjoyed the sport. You have hobbies?"

"I like to clean up old motorcycles. I'm trying to learn a little bit of each discipline for construction.

Last few months concrete. This week I started on plumbing."

"That sounds fun. Very *This Old House* kind of a hobby."

"What do you look for most in a date?" He cleared his throat. "Just so I know what expectations to strive for."

"I like to play by the rules. Coffee first. Dinner. If we like each other, we call right away—none of that wait two days game playing. Honesty."

His face—though he kept it neutral—twitched for a second and Mary wondered if she'd imagined it. "You're not a rules guy?" she guessed.

"Where would you get that idea? I love rules." He leaned in close, amusement in his voice. "If we don't have rules then there's no fun when I find ways to break them."

"Some rules…we should break. Some topics are going to be deal breakers. More than toilet paper."

He nodded, not saying anything for a moment, and she wondered what side of the fence Calvin landed on as far as the gun debate and if she should dive into those questions so soon. She decided to go for broke and ask. "Calvin…"

He squinted and tilted his head to the side. "My name isn't Calvin. It's…Henry." He paused as if he weren't sure himself. "People call me Hank." He'd added on that nickname with more confidence.

"Oh." Mary shuffled the same two steps they'd been instructed to practice, the monotony of the repeated moves making it easier to carry the conversation and give them something to do other than stare at each other awkwardly. Though they were doing a fine job not making the whole dating experiment weird.

He stopped dancing for a beat, glancing at Dr. Miles. He swung her to the far side of the dance floor as far away as they could possibly get from their love researcher. "Your name isn't Annette."

She shook her head, finally realizing the confusion. "It's Mary. Mary Amble."

He swung her around so his back would be to the researcher and closed his eyes. "Shit."

Mary's shoulder sunk. Something had gone wrong. She wasn't the woman he'd been expecting. He'd already checked her off his list. Of course. She was being stood up again, in real time. Good thing she didn't get her hopes up. He covered the disappointment quickly. "I'm sorry," she said, her voice sounding small even to her own ears.

Just like that, the date she didn't want to have twenty minutes ago didn't want her either. Right when she'd piqued an interest in the guy. Good thing she didn't get too attached.

Shit. Shit. Shit. Hank was on the wrong date. The wrong name. Wrong time. It all made sense that the mix-up had happened. Mary's date didn't show, and he wandered in like a goof because he didn't know the protocol for this love in a test tube thing…considering he was an imposter. He panicked while he tried not to panic. Not the best strategy for alluding anxiety. If he told her now, before they had a connection, would she "Nope" out of the deal? Honesty. She'd asked him for exactly that a few seconds ago and he'd already messed that one up before he even made it through the door. He never expected when he started his morning that he'd meet someone he wanted to see again. He wanted the opportunity to keep knowing her, if she wanted the same. They weren't officially a match on paper. Then again, that wouldn't be the case either way since he'd agreed to this scheme for Henry's sake.

"I was in the army, too," he said instead. "Just like your dad."

She perked up. A good sign. "Angling for an introduction to my parents?" Her smile was shaky and uncertain, but since she'd attempted to keep things light, he would too. Maybe she didn't have any idea about the mix up. Should he play this out and let the researcher discover it on his own then hit Mary up for her number after? They could laugh it off over a coffee. The coffee could become dinner next week if things went well.

"Doesn't the camera crew follow us to a hometown date in episode eight?" he joked.

Her smile was real this time. "That's a reality TV show. This is science."

"Well then, science." His bit his cheek. "Make it by date five then."

Her expression went serious. "So I guess if you were in the army then you're pro-gun?"

He weighed his answer, hoping she wasn't a gun nut. "The military use them for protection. I have

one that I keep locked in a safe. I never have reason to take it out. I've considered selling it actually. I've never been into the things." He watched her carefully.

"Me either." She hesitated. "Except for the sport aspect."

"Skeet has always sounded like fun. Tell you what. If you ever want to show me…I can promise you I'll be more coordinated than dancing. Let's leave it at that."

"We'll have to do that some time. I have a teacher's schedule, so spring break is coming up."

"I'd love that." He quickly returned to the other tidbit she'd offered about herself. "Teaching, yeah?"

She nodded.

"What subject?"

"Grade level," she corrected. "Fourth grade. You?"

He inwardly cringed at her innocent question. He'd been between jobs and bartending nights to keep up with bills. "I'm exploring options. I was in construction, but things got slow, so I picked up some side stuff to fill in the gaps. Bartending mostly."

"Thinking about going back to school?" She asked it in a non-threatening way, a way he could easily agree and not seem like a louse. "With the hobbies you listed earlier all being construction it seems like the natural step to want to work toward a license and some formal training. They have great programs for veterans at Curie Tech."

"Do they? I'm interested." He thought it over and realized he wasn't merely giving her what she wanted to hear. He wanted to go to school. Always had, but there was usually money on the table with some job project and he'd chosen the money offered now rather than the potential in his future. This slowdown in his life—she'd seen it as an opportunity. He liked that.

Their instructor flew back into the room. "Excellent. Your steps are already improving. I should leave you to practice more often! Mary and Calvin, about ready to enter professional competition soon. Don't you say, Miles?"

He researcher popped his head up from his paperwork. "I'll second that!"

Mary turned them to face the teacher but didn't—Hank noted—take her hand from his. The tingle of awareness had kept him hard. A state he didn't plan on letting her in on for fear of being taken as a creep on their first "date." He wanted to know if she felt it too—the connection, not the, uh, other thing. He gave her hand the slightest squeeze. She returned it, her lips turning up slightly with a sparkle in her eyes when she shyly glanced his way and back to the instructor.

The untruth he'd failed to tell her settled in his gut and festered. *Honesty.*

Not one to miss a minute of school. *Rule follower.* Not at all like the usual women he ended up with, that's for sure. Except she was everything he'd wanted and didn't have the courage to go after himself. She gave him confidence. Her talking to him like he was her equal, he knew that if things didn't work out with them, his first order of business was to enroll himself into classes and get that college degree he'd wanted. Become the person she seemed to see in him.

They moved the lesson to another kind of dance and this time Hank paid close attention. Concentrating in each move and following the instructor's body positions so he could understand the steps. He made for a terrible dancer, but damn, it had been fun.

With Mary. That made the difference.

Honesty. The reminder of what he'd been keeping from her snaked into each breath. He couldn't keep this up.

They took a brief break and he followed Mary over to the snacks while the instructor and the researcher huddled on the sidelines, giving them privacy. Hank decided this was his best opportunity to let Mary in on the discovery he figured out earlier. "Don't react. Just listen to what I have to say and hear me out. You know I like to break the rules and I have a proposal for you."

Mary's eyes widened. Yesh, he could have been less secret-agent about it all. Now he'd spooked her.

"My name isn't Calvin and yours isn't Annette. My date isn't officially for another half-hour…" he let the last trail off so she would come to the conclusion herself.

"We're both on the wrong date. With each other." Her eyes closed as she came to the realization. "That was what you figured out while we were dancing."

"Yeah."

"I'm sorry—you must be wanting to clear things up with Dr. Miles so you can get to the person you were matched with." Her gaze wouldn't meet his.

"That's the thing. I don't think I could go on that date. Not after meeting you." He fumbled for the right words. "That is…if you feel the same…"

Her eyes fluttered and she glanced at their researcher overlord. "But there's a test and a background check, and an interview. They've carefully selected what works in a relationship and what doesn't—"

"I didn't take any of those. Who's to say that we wouldn't have been matched if I *had* gone through all those hoops? This is where I'm asking you to break a few rules."

"But…how?" She frowned, catching on that little bit of information Hank should have kept to himself but couldn't. He wouldn't start dating someone under false pretenses. And the short time he knew Mary he had been positive she wouldn't start a relationship under these conditions either. "I need to stay in the study for insurance…wait, how did you get in if you didn't do the paperwork?"

"I'm filling in for a friend. He has the same name as me: Henry Jones. He had the flu and couldn't afford to be dropped from the study." Hank shrugged.

Mary's hand went to her cheek. "Okay. Wow." She kept her voice low. "It's a little weird. You could be a serial killer."

"Yeah. I could." He agreed solemnly. "Or I could be your soul mate?"

She poked him in the chest playfully. "Now don't get ahead of yourself."

"We won't know unless we spend some more time together. Somewhere not here." He glanced at the dance teacher and Dr. Miles. "Somewhere public. Meet me at the coffee shop on the corner of Emily Roebling Road and Lamarr Street."

"I know it. It's just that the study has rules about outside dating. If it becomes serious…"

"Let's not think about that yet. Think about what I'll order for you. Favorite coffee?"

"Herbal tea. But I—"

"If you don't show, it's a no. It's okay. Either way. I understand. I'm sorry I didn't tell you right away. I'll wait until your tea goes cold to be sure."

He didn't have an opportunity to make any further plans. The instructor interrupted them and now was his chance to set his plan in motion. He'd either never see her again or they would make a fresh start.

"Let's see if we can try that first dance again—"

He put his hand over his stomach and rubbed. "I'm—I think I ate something that didn't agree with me."

Mary's eyebrows flew up with concern. "Are you going to be okay? Hank? Do you still want to meet—"

"I should go," he cut her off with a pointed look and hoped she got his secret message—*We're still meeting*—before she gave away their plans as the researcher rose from his seat and checked the clipboard. "This was lovely. I'll e-mail and see what the next steps are?" He called to the researcher as he backed his way to the door. "Will you tell the next date? Let her know so she doesn't have to wait like Mary did," he added on to the end. Because standing someone up was a crap move. He wouldn't let someone go through it if he could help it. "The name's Henry Jones, by the way. Check your computers. That will explain it."

He left before too many questions could be asked. Then he darted through the rain to the coffee shop to order Mary's tea and make a wish it wouldn't get cold waiting for her.

Mary gathered her purse and coat, pressing her hand into her temple. What happened? Calvin was Hank, Hank was pretending to be Henry. She liked the guy. Had a good feeling from him, regardless of all the crazy events surrounding the ordeal, and he seemed genuinely concerned about the mix up. He wanted her to break some rules and for once the idea excited her. A little adventure for love.

Dr. Miles slid his fingers across his tablet and squinted, making all kinds of oh-shit faces at whatever results his screen had manifested for him. He scrubbed a hand down his face. "This is my fault. I pulled him from the elevator, and he tried to tell me his name and show his ID, but I shoved him into the date because I was so concerned about him being late. I didn't realize he was early." The doctor's gaze met hers. "For another date."

"You both seemed to hit it off," the dance instructor said. Holding her elbow across her torso, she bit her lip and watched Mary and the researcher carefully. "Did he seem interested in another date?"

"He said he was," Mary admitted, but didn't want to give the details in case it would get them in trouble. Best not open that beehive just yet.

"Maybe if…." The instructor let the end of her thought hang as she glanced to Dr. Miles for direction.

Miles shook his head. "I'd have to run the numbers. And he didn't fill out his exit sheet. I'll have to call or e-mail him to go over the date and his thoughts."

But Mary had a feeling that if he did that, he'd realize Hank wasn't who he claimed to be. There appeared to be a reason why Hank wanted to keep it secret, and she wouldn't know unless she met with him. Being in a tight insurance bind herself, she didn't want to mess up Hank's friend either. "I should get going." She hitched her purse strap onto her shoulder.

Dr. Miles tucked his tablet under his arm. "I'm so sorry. This has been a terrible breach of protocol and I'm to blame."

"No, it was fine. I had a good time." She turned to the instructor. "I've always wanted to learn."

"Come by my studio for a free lesson. On me." The woman handed over her business card and a look of sympathy she couldn't hide flashed across her face. "I remember dating. It was a horrible, terrible time."

Pity. That look had been pity. The instructor must have thought her date bailed because of some flaw he saw in her. Mary pasted on her best fake smile. "It's an adventure."

She walked to the exit, still unsure if she would take a detour a few blocks over to the little coffee shop Hank mentioned, or go home and call her sister to decompress over the weirdest hour she'd experienced in a long time.

"Oh wait," the dance instructor called out. "You forgot your debriefing sheet." The woman jogged after her in her too-high heels and Mary stopped, twisting around to grab the sheet and get the hell out of there and down to the coffee shop where she'd get answers. Or an empty table because Hank really did have a stomachache.

Except Mary couldn't shake that feeling he felt what she had. A connection.

The instructor wobbled, not expecting Mary to turn so abruptly, and she stepped to the side and one of her graceful feet landed squarely on the floor vent. Her heel snapping. Her ankle cracking.

Holy…that sound it made had been unexpected. "Oh my gosh!" Mary knelt to the ground where the woman sprawled in attempt to keep her foot at the correct angle. "Are you okay?"

The dance instructor breathed in quick snaps. It reminded Mary of actresses on television mimicking Lamaze while giving birth. "My foot. My foot. My foot." The woman said over and over. Her eyes getting wider, staring at the injury.

Dr. Miles cursed and flew past them to the phones. "Maxwell? It's me. Send someone from medical right away!"

Then they both rushed to the instructor's side to see if they could do anything to mitigate the damage, but that ankle swelled, promising them it wasn't going to be a simple fix.

Mary couldn't leave. The instructor squeezed her hand. "I can't dance. I'll never be able to dance again!"

All Mary could think about was she might never get a chance to catch Hank. He'd never know what delayed her and assume she'd said no to the get-to-know-me date. He made it clear he wouldn't bother her, and since she knew Hank was filling in for his friend, she may never know how to contact him. The study made it clear they took safety protocols seriously. Nobody would be allowed to communicate outside of the experiment until both parties fully consented, and that wouldn't be allowed until a few dates had taken place. She and Hank were clearly breaking several rules by attempting this coffee thing.

Well, that didn't look like it would be a problem anymore anyway. Considering she wasn't going to be doing any rule breaking any time soon. Not when she seemed to be supervising a medical emergency.

Hank checked the clock again. It had been a full forty minutes. Plenty of time for Mary to make an escape. Her tea was still warm, so there was hope. He'd put it in two insulated sleeves and asked them to make it extra hot. And he promised he'd stay until it was cold. He could give her a few more minutes. Just in case…

He also knew he had work to do. Business to take care of before he could date Mary with a clear con-science. He texted Henry to get the ball rolling on that front.

Hey buddy. I know you asked me for a favor in going on this date for you, I'm about to ask you for an even bigger one…

Mary rushed across the street. God, she'd hit every single DON'T WALK sign and had to stop for every bicyclist and slow-moving mother with her children. The older lady with a walker asking her for directions was a bit much—though she couldn't resist escorting the woman to her lawyer's office with how bad the roads were. The rain kicked back up and she held her umbrella over the woman as they walked.

Now she finally had the coffee shop in sight. Mary peeked into the tall glass windows, searching each table for the auburn-haired man in a leather jacket and the unexpected charm. Unable to spot him, she jerked the door open and the bells ringed with a ding-a-ling. She slowly paced around each table, looking at each customer, until she came across one with a full cup. Extra liners around the side, it clearly marked the name Hank—a coffee shop miracle it had been spelled right—and yep, the receipt stuck under it said "herbal special—mint, lavender, and rosehips."

Mary swallowed, her fingers gripping around the cup. It had grown cold. She flagged down a barista. "Excuse me?" The guy looked over at her, pausing his wipe down of the work counter. "Where did the man go who was sitting here?"

Really? What a silly question—of course he wouldn't know. The place was packed—

"The guy that waited for an hour." He made a face to let her know exactly how he felt about late people. *Believe me, buddy, I hear ya*, she wanted to say. "He just left." The guy pointed out the back door which led to courtyard into the university.

Mary waved her thanks and ran the direction he pointed.

Hank knew the moment his phone rang that Henry had followed through on his promise. Dr. Miles seemed like a thorough researcher and would be horrified at the breach that Henry and he created with their switch. Either way, he'd asked Mary to break the rules by going on this date. He'd wanted the next step to be for him to follow the rules to make it even for them, but that wouldn't matter now that she hadn't shown.

He let the call go to voicemail. He'd deal with it later. Much later, after a shower, dry clothes, and a beer. Shoving his phone into his pocket he swung his leg around his motorcycle, set his boot to start it, but instead of the rev of the engine he heard a familiar voice call out, "Wait! Hank!"

Hank squinted through the rain dripping down his face to see Mary avoiding puddles and shuffling through the uneven pavers to the motorcycle parking. "Great moves there. Did you ever consider taking dance lessons?"

She snorted. "Very funny."

He sat back against his seat. "I thought maybe you'd changed your mind." She had needed the insurance. A detail they'd need to figure out if this date went well.

"Did you change yours? You said you wanted me to take you skeet shooting."

He glanced at the sky and the evidence of uncooperative weather.

"I know a place where the rain won't be an issue," she said as if she'd read his mind.

"I might be up for that."

"You sure you feel up to it? After the way you bailed saying you ate something that didn't agree with you—"

He crossed his arms. "You got me. I lied. But only because I didn't want to keep stepping on your nice shoes."

She rolled her eyes and tipped her chin, instructing him to follow. He smiled, very glad for his second chance.

"Broke her ankle?" Hank set his plastic laser gun down, missing the digital duck that flashed across the computer screen. A little cartoon dog came up and laughed at him. He glared at it for making him look like an idiot in front of the chick he'd been trying to impress. "Tricky bastard."

"Don't say that about Gallery the dog. He's got papers, so I'm sure his mother and father were properly wed." Mary set her gun up, using her wrist to steady her shot. She pinged the two ducks presented on her first turn.

"Show off," Hank said, and took a sip of his beer. The empty pizza boxes had been set by the now over-flowing trash can, so he got up and gestured to it. "Where's your main garbage bin? I'll take this out."

Mary glanced at it. Hitting the two ducks again. "Don't worry about it. I invited you over to hang out, not to clean."

"It's no problem. I might as well make myself useful while you hunt us up a second dinner." He gathered up the items, pulling the larger black plastic liner out and shoving the boxes inside. He glanced up at the fridge, grinning at her organized calendar. "You have book release dates on your calendar."

"You bet!" she said. "And if that kind of forethought scares you then don't look at my planner."

"Of course you have a planner." He peeked at the next question on the list taped to the fridge. "Hey," he said. "Favorite season?"

They'd been doing this since they'd sneaked off to continue their date, asking questions and going down the check list of "relationship building exercises" Mary had gotten on her handout from the experiment. It had started as a joke and then became more of an interest, waiting for some random item to convince them they were crazy for getting along so easily.

There had to be something. So far the only thing keeping them apart was the fact that Hank would be booted from the experiment for impersonating a participant. Mary had already explained to him again she needed to stay in the study for insurance reasons.

Mary popped three ducks in a row for her grand finale and then set her plastic gun on the coffee table. "Spring. When the cherry trees are blooming."

"Fall," he answered. "The leaves change colors."

"Is that a bad thing?" She pretended to be scared, clawing at her arms and coming to join him in the small little kitchen unit. "We like different seasons."

"Could have been much worse. I hear marriages between winter and summer people don't last more than a few weeks." Hank nodded solemnly.

She laughed that time, a full-of-life sound that Hank wanted to make happen again.

"Worst date." Mary countered with the next discussion topic.

"Easy. Sixth grade. Karah—with a 'k' and an 'h'— make sure you spell it right. She wanted to go to a party and be wild, so she promised me she'd get me an A on my next paper if I took her to one and made her feel cool for a night. I didn't really need the A. I had a solid C in the class, but the inflection in her tone lead me to believe that she could just as easily fail me if I refused and Mr. Guillard, the teacher she was a TA for, would believe her word over mine in a heartbeat."

"So I'm guessing you took her and it was awful."

"Not exactly. She actually was fine once she light-ened up. We messed around a little. I thought… maybe—that is until she went exclusive with Johna-than Langston the very next day. Turns out it was all to impress him."

"Real bummer."

"You?" Hank asked, wondering who would be dumb enough to treat her badly.

"I'd have to have gone on a date recently to say. I keep getting stood up."

Hank frowned. "You're kidding me."

She shook her head. "Nope. Wish I was kidding so I don't sound lame."

"They're the lame ones."

Her smile didn't reach her eyes. "True story. Lat-est lame guy? We were set up by a colleague. It was supposed to be mini golf on Valentine's Day. I sat in the cafe with my putter and ball for forty min-utes. Texted my colleague to see what might have happened and she acted surprised. Turns out they hooked up instead. She's been avoiding me the last few weeks."

"That counts as a terrible date."

"I didn't go on a date though." Mary poked his side and he didn't flinch in hopes she would try it again.

They'd tip-toed around the main topic all after-noon. Mary would need to keep herself available for the experiment. Hank wouldn't be a part of that. He'd already explained himself to Miles in an e-mail he sent while he waited for Mary. He'd been too afraid to check his replies. He shoved those thoughts aside, deciding instead to be in the moment with Mary. She'd brought the topic up a few times, but he'd suc-cessfully changed the subject.

Mary crossed off the question from her print out, her cheeks reddening on the next items. Hank knew

what she'd spotted. The sheet moved from general knowledge to sexual chemistry exercises. The sheet encouraged participants to touch, stare into each other's eyes, kiss.

He had to admit he was looking forward to that one. He set the trash back down by the back door and tentatively reached for her hand on the counter. The touch zinged like before. A flutter in his nervous system that made him feel a hundred pounds lighter and slightly dizzy. He stroked his thumb down hers and her shiver told him she felt it too. Their eyes met and their breathing kicked into a higher rhythm.

"We shouldn't," Mary whispered.

"Do you want to?"

She shook her head, closing her eyes. "God, yes."

Hank leaned in close, knowing he could take those last few inches and she wouldn't stop him. She wouldn't protest. Her mouth opened, welcoming.

His phone rang again. It had been going off all afternoon. Likely Henry. Either angry at Hank or chagrined over the situation they were all in. It didn't matter because the spell of the moment had been broken and Mary eased back, mumbling some-thing about laundry.

Hank hoisted up the trash and headed for the larger bin outside. He mashed his finger on the call accept square on his screen. "What, asshole."

"Oh, Mr. Jones?" a voice he could barely place said on the other line. "This is Dr. Miles. I'm so sorry about earlier."

"It's…" *Fine* he'd almost said. "Did you get my e-mail?"

"I did. I understand you're not the Henry Jones we have on file. You were filling in for a friend? You purposefully mislead a date."

He hated admitting it out loud again, hearing the details spoken so boldly. "Yeah."

"Mary is a wonderful person. She didn't deserve this."

"No. I agree." Hank's gaze turned to the light glow-ing in the window of her house. "That's why I told her as soon as I realized we were on the wrong date."

"She marked you as highly compatible and that she would like to see you again on another date in her debriefing interview."

"She did?" He couldn't help but get a little excited. Sure, Mary ended up continuing the date in secret with him, but it still felt good to hear it.

"Too bad you're not in the study to go on that second date," Dr. Miles tsked.

"I…yeah. Again, really sorry. Is there some kind of fine I have to pay? I could fork over some cash for the dance lessons and snacks you provided."

"It's just too bad you're not in the study is all," Miles repeated again, his tone more hinting than the last time he'd said it.

It didn't take Hank long to catch on to that one. "What do I need to do?"

Dr. Miles rattled off a few questions and instructions on how to take the online tests. Hank gave verbal approval for a background test and gave his credit card to pay for the expedited results. Dr. Miles explained that there was no guarantee he'd be accepted as a participant and not to count on it.

"I know you've done a lot already by fixing this for me," Hank said. "But I have one last favor. It's about the activity for our next date. If I get approved."

He explained to Dr. Miles the background, not giving away that he and Mary had broken a few rules of the experiment already, but it sounded like ones in place for safety more than experiment integrity.

"It's unorthodox, and you'll be going about this relationship in the wrong order for our experiment parameters. I'll have to write a footnote after to explain the data inconsistency issues." The researcher muttered to himself. "All right. I'll set your next date up for tomorrow morning contingent on your paperwork going through and send Mary an e-mail to see if she'd like to go on another date."

He hung up and started the compatibility test on his phone, just as he'd promised Miles he would. He rushed through it, not realizing how long the thing was. Jesus.

Mary came out after a half hour. "Hank?"

He glanced up from the glow of his screen. "Hey. I—I had something I had to do, so I thought I'd—" He saved his progress and shoved the phone into his pocket. "I can finish it up later."

Mary bit her lip and hugged herself. "Right. Listen—" Her voice changed, going low. She must have already read the e-mail from Dr. Miles. "I was thinking…I should quit the study. We kinda messed things up and I should have—"

Hank rushed to her, bringing her into his arms and noting how easily they fit together, even after only knowing each other for a few hours. "Hey. No. Look, I want you to keep at it. You need the insurance. I wouldn't ask you to make that choice. I like you. A lot. I want to pull the planner off your fridge and schedule myself in for nights and weekends like you said wanted while we danced—"

She kissed him. No warning. No hesitation. Just bam. Right there. His fingers spread in surprise on her biceps and then when his brain caught up, he pulled her in tighter. Their lips started fast, hurried, desperate. Then he changed the angle and they slowed. Passion. Sensation. His mouth explored hers. She pulled back first, and he missed her already. The kiss had been a more of a goodbye than a hello.

"I don't want to stay in the study," Mary said again, this time with her hands on his chest, gripping his shirt like she wouldn't let go, but her fists pressing as if she would push him away anyway. "But I have a medical thing…" She eased away. "I barely know you. This is weird. I feel like I don't have enough information to make an informed decision and no matter what decision I make I'll regret it if it doesn't work."

Hank understood. He nearly told her his plan but didn't want to get her hopes up. Miles had said he can't guarantee him a spot. But Hank had faith. He pulled her close for a hug. This time she flattened her fists and slide her hands around him, holding tight.

He kissed her forehead. "I should go."

She nodded, covering her face and backing away. He didn't want her to choose between her health or some guy she'd just met who crashed her date. It wasn't fair to ask her to quit the study over *some guy*, granted, even if *that guy* was him. He moved slowly to his motorcycle, gripping the handlebars. The throaty engine was the worst sound he could imagine as he sped off into the night.

Mary regretted her decision instantly and the bags under her eyes from a sleepless night were a fairly good indication of that. She'd tossed and turned, wishing she'd asked for Hank's phone number at the very least. Or a plan for a second date. Or a hint it would be okay for him to come check on her in a month or so if the experiment spit her out because none of the other participants she'd matched with wanted a second date. Dr. Miles had sent her an email explaining the issue she already knew about with Hank: He wasn't a participant when he attended the date. All the data from their date would be scrapped. He wanted to make it up to her with another date that would be recorded in its place. Someone who scored high enough on the compatibility scale with her that he felt it would be worth setting up a date between them.

High enough. God. It sounded like long shot. There was only one Hank. She wanted an ex-ar-my-bartending-going-back-to-school guy who did things like crash researching dates for a friend with the flu and she never seemed to run out of things to talk about with. That guy had been hard to find and when she found him, he seemed into her. He wouldn't let her drop her chance at the insurance. She wanted *that* guy.

She parked her car at the designated meeting place. This time it wasn't scheduled at the research offices but out in public. Miles had said that some dates would be around town and he would "shadow" the participants for notes on body language.

She waved at the researcher when she saw him standing out front. Miles made an "ah-ha" face when he spotted her and positioned himself to stand right in front of her car while she parked. Mary did her best to rally herself into a better, more excited mood than the one she was in. Dr. Miles was trying hard to find her a match. She could at least do her part and be open to the ones he presented.

"I think you'll like this one. He's very serious about finding *just* the right person," the researcher said in place of a greeting.

Mary fumbled to grab her purse from behind her seat, her door open, and she set one leg on the pavement. She swallowed down the ball of guilt forming in her throat. Guilt hurt. She couldn't shake the fact that she felt like she was betraying someone by being here. That someone being Hank.

She got her purse, setting it in her lap. Then stared out the front window, unable to convince the rest of her body to follow through with this plan. Yeah, she knew what was right. She knew whoever she saw on this date she wouldn't be giving them a full chance. She needed space. She needed to track down Hank.

"I'm making a mistake," Mary said, shocked she'd spoken out loud, but once it was out there, she couldn't take it back.

Dr. Mile's eyes widened. "I assure you I'm very sorry about yesterday, but—"

"No. You can't be sorry about that. I'm glad for that date, but it made me realize what I wanted and what I want is to find Hank. Could you reach out to Henry Jones and ask him—"

"Henry Jones dropped himself from the program. Something about marrying his sweetheart to get on her insurance plan." Dr. Miles scanned the parking lot as if he were searching for snipers and whipped out his phone, frantically texting.

The news of the marriage stabbed at her gut before she realized it wasn't her Henry Jones he was talking about. "I'm glad he's got it figured out, but I'm begging you—"

"I can't contact Henry Jones." Dr. Miles shook his head. "However, I really think you'd be interested in this date."

She clutched her purse, bringing her foot back into her car. "It's not a good idea. Tell whoever it is that I'm so sorry. I know what it's like to be stood up, but tell them I connected more with another date and just realizing I might need space before I jump right back in—"

"Mary!"

She startled at the shout of her name from a familiar voice. Her fingers poised on pressing the ignition button on her Prius. "Hank?"

Then she spotted him, running toward her car from inside. Was that a golf club in his hand?

"Mary, wait." He huffed as he caught his breath.

Dr. Miles took over. "I can explain. I showed your date video to my partners and they all agreed that your chemistry and spark scales were perfect. We'd hate to abandon this relationship when it clearly has some potential. The two of you are, well, I don't want to jinx it, but we want to see where you go from here. And we need more dates to be certain."

"You joined the study?" Mary asked, her brain not catching up to the excitement that vibrated through her. "How?"

"It was a test, a background check…all that stuff you told me at our lesson." He held up his golf club. "I heard some idiot stood you up on Valentine's Day.

I don't know about you, but a good game of mini golf is hard to pass up if your aim is anywhere close to what it is on Duck Hunt—"

Mary sprang from the car, knocking Hank back a foot. His arms wrapped around her and she felt warm for the first time since he let go last night. "I made a huge mistake by letting you go."

"Clearly not," the researcher interrupted. "If you'd both dropped from this study, we would have lost a potential success story to tout to our investors."

"And you would have lost your insurance plan," Hank whispered to her.

"I would have lost you," Mary said.

"You didn't." He tucked her closer, keeping his voice low. "I would have found a way. You didn't have to choose. I wanted that for you."

They held each other for a little longer and Dr. Miles moved away to give them some privacy.

She arched an eyebrow, shooting a look to Hank's club. "Well, I'm glad to see you're on time."

"Not by my calculations," he grinned. "I'm late. Late in taking so long to meet you. If we'd meet a few weeks sooner, you wouldn't have had that horrible Valentine's Day."

"Then why don't we re-write it. You're my Valentine's date. And I never let you walk away after our first date."

"We did make a day of it."

"In the retelling we made a night of it."

"I like this version." Hank wiggled his eyebrows and handed over his club. "Well, Mary, let's see what you got."

And they had the best late Valentine's Day date Mary had ever had, and not just because she won the first round of mini golf.

L. Penelope has been writing since she could hold a pen and loves getting lost in the worlds in her head. She is an award-winning fantasy and paranormal romance author. She lives in Maryland with her husband and their furry dependents. Sign up for new release information, updates, and giveaways on her website: http://www.lpenelope.com.

BEFORE I BREAK

Part One

by L. Penelope

CHAPTER ONE

Luce spun in the swivel chair, her sensible heels lightly skimming the linoleum. The lunch rush rioted around her in a pastel blur. She embraced the dizziness—she felt more in control knowing she could simply plant her feet on the ground and the world would right itself. Few things in life were that simple.

A small, static figure set apart from the whirling din caused her to skid to a stop. The little boy, four or five years old, whose mouth and cheeks were smudged with what she suspected was cherry chocolate from Delilah's Candy Bar just across the courtyard, stood staring at Luce. She rolled her chair closer and leaned down.

"Do you need help?"

He blinked a few times and licked at the chocolate still coating his lips.

"It seems this little guy is lost," a voice rumbled from above.

She shifted her gaze to the right and encountered a pair of scuffed black boots. Directly above them were sturdy canvas pants, a plaid button-up shirt, and the pièce de résistance—Mathias Woodson's movie star-worthy face, the corners of his mouth turned up in a smile.

Great.

She stood, though even in her professional, patent leather, slightly squishy heels, she was no match for his height. Still, she straightened her pencil skirt and cleared her throat. *Close your mouth, remember to breathe, blink, and for God's sake don't stare.*

After two months of working with him, she still had to run through the checklist every time she encountered the man. She refused to be like the gaggle of women trailing after him, drooling at his feet.

Though she'd checked off all the most likely areas of possible embarrassment, she could only hold his gaze for a moment before retreating to the safety of considering the little boy. "What's your name, sweetheart?"

A blank stare was the only response. She shot a questioning glance to Mat, who shrugged. "I think he took the whole 'don't talk to strangers' thing to heart."

"Superb."

The little boy was adorable—dark curly hair, suntoasted bronze skin. In fact, he and Mat could have been brothers, or father and son, they looked so much alike. Luce scanned the area for desperate parents searching for their missing child.

Lost kids were part of the territory when manning the information booth at the Button Factory. The shopping center-slash-tourist trap at Fisherman's Wharf in San Francisco had been an actual button-producing factory up until the mid-1960s. After a few decades of neglect, the building was renovated and repurposed and now featured three levels of shopping and dining. Tourists from all over the world packed the brick building, and the first floor info booth was at the center of it all.

Luce had first gotten the job in college when she'd been a hospitality major. She liked people and loved talking to travelers from the countries she'd always dreamed of visiting. Though she'd eventually changed her major to public relations and gotten promoted after graduation to work in the Factory's business office on the fourth floor, she looked forward to days like today when she was asked to fill in for an absent co-worker.

With another look at the cherubic, chocolate-covered face, Luce picked up the intercom and called the security office to put their guards on alert for the parents. When she hung up, Mat was kneeling down, wiping the boy's mouth with a wet nap he'd produced from somewhere.

The boy, fairly stoic up until then, looked around with a freshly clean face and burst into tears. Mat's eyes widened. He turned to Luce, silently pleading for help with the bawling child. She sighed and sat back in her chair, then lifted the boy into her lap.

"Your mommy and daddy will be here soon. I bet they're looking everywhere for you right now." As she tried to encourage him, a cold fear sliced her belly. She hoped her words weren't lies. All parents were not created equal, as she well knew.

She spun him around in the chair a few times, racking her brain for something to calm him down. His T-shirt featured a colorful image of the caboose of a train.

"Do you like trains?"

He sniffed a few times before nodding.

"Have you ever been on a real train before?"

He shook his head.

"Neither have I, unless you count BART—that's the subway—but I don't. One day I'm going to take a train trip and sit right up front near the engine. Wouldn't that be fun?"

The boy cracked a smile. "Thomas is a train engine."

"You're right!"

Mat squatted down. "I've been on lots of trains and they are really fun. I took a train in India that had goats and chickens walking down the aisles."

The kid's eyes widened and Mat nodded.

"The smell was terrible."

Mat held his nose, and the boy broke out into an infectious round of giggles. Luce couldn't help but smile, though she dropped it when Mat winked at her. He then launched into a tale that involved a goat, his favorite T-shirt, and a tug of war that didn't end well.

Those definitely were not her ovaries brawling inside of her, vying for first crack at this delightful specimen of man. She clenched her belly and willed her ladybits to calm the hell down. There really wasn't anything to get excited about.

When she looked up, Randy, one of the security guards, was approaching ahead of a rather calm looking man and woman, both impeccably dressed.

"Freddy," said an exasperated, statuesque blonde with an expensive-looking haircut. "You're going to make us miss our bus to Napa. Do you know how expensive those tickets were?" She spoke with a European accent Luce couldn't place.

The father, a short, roly poly man with skin a shade darker than Luce's own ebony complexion, spoke in a heavy Jamaican accent. "Dat boy don't have da sense he was born with. And look, him run off wit da candy and ate it all!"

As she stood, settling Freddy to his feet, Luce schooled her features, masking her anger. Suddenly she was seven years old again, swinging her legs on the metal chair of a hotel's security office, pretending to watch the cartoons on the television the kind guards had set her in front of. Hours later, when her parents finally returned for her, they'd chastised *her* for making them miss their bus and resulting in a change fee for new tickets. Was it too much to ask that your own parents not check out and leave their daughter behind?

Her eyes stung as tears threatened from the long-buried memory. She clenched her jaw, looked away and held her breath. Counted to ten. She'd been in the service industry long enough to know how to keep from strangling the customers.

When she'd regained her composure and looked up, Mat was peering at her. Luce plastered on a professionally plastic smile.

Randy went through the procedures to ensure that these in fact were the parents and not some strange kidnappers, but the boy's joy at seeing the couple was obvious, even as they berated him.

"I expect you to behave, Freddy. You know we could have taken this trip by ourselves and not had half of the hassles. I told you—"

"First time in San Francisco?" Luce asked, rocking slightly on the balls of her feet.

The woman looked up mid-diatribe, as if surprised to see Luce standing there. "Yes, I've always wanted to come, but Vernon has very little time off." She patted her husband's arm, but his attention was firmly on the window display of Delilah's Candy Bar across the way.

"I'm glad you could make the trip. There's so much to see. And where are you from?"

"Norway, originally. But we've been in London for the past few years."

"Oh really? My mother's from Norway," Mat said. The woman raised her eyebrows and ran her eyes down his body. Slowly. Her thorough scan was both skeptical and lascivious. Luce bristled.

A string of foreign words flowed from Mat's mouth. If that was Norwegian, it sounded like a language that belonged on a space ship. The woman responded, and the two pelted each other in rapid-fire Norwegian for a minute.

Mat bent down and whispered to Freddy. The boy nodded, grinning big. Then the family walked off, the boy scurrying to keep up with his parents' long strides.

"What did you say to him?" Luce asked.

"I told him to be careful of the goats on the cable cars."

Mat's eyes twinkled. Luce shook her head and forced herself to look away. Then took a step back. Standing next to him, breathing in his clean, masculine scent was too much. She ran through her checklist once again and busied herself straightening the brochures in the overflowing rack.

"How much longer are you stuck down here?" His voice rippled over her skin and she actually shivered.

"Um, Nora's shift starts in five minutes. She should be here any second. But I don't feel stuck. I kind of like it. The grass is always greener," she chuckled. "When I was down here all I wanted was to make it up there." She tilted her head to the exposed levels of the open courtyard. The offices where they worked were on the fourth floor. "Now I miss the noise, the activity." She shrugged.

"I don't think I could take it." He scanned the crowded tables and lines at the food vendors and shook his head slightly.

"You'd rather be cooped up in front of a computer all day staring at pixels? You might call your job graphic design, but I call it slow torture. Give me the unwashed masses any day. Besides, I would have thought you'd be used to them, with as much traveling as you seem to have done."

"Yeah, I like to observe, not really interact. And the questions you get here…" He trailed off as an irate man stalked to the booth, a sniffling woman in tow.

"She said she wanted to go to Alcatraz." He slapped his hand on the counter. "How could she not know she'd have to take a boat there? It's an island for Chrissakes!"

The pair had the look of newlyweds, with their matching T-shirts and cargo shorts. The young wife dabbed her eyes. "I get seasick," she said softly.

"Well, I already bought the damn tickets! You couldn't have told me about that before?"

"Listen," Luce said, holding the husband's eye. "There's a ticket exchange across the street at the pier." She pulled out a map and highlighted the location. "Go here and you can find someone who wants to go to Alcatraz to take your tickets and you can change them out for something else, maybe a walking tour or a trip to Coit Tower." Luce smiled at the wife.

"I'm afraid of heights," she whispered. Her husband groaned, throwing up his hands in frustration.

"Well, there are lots of other options," Luce said, evenly. "I'm sure you can find something to do that doesn't involve water or heights."

The couple walked away, the man grumbling, the woman cowering. Luce fell into her chair with a sigh, pointedly not looking at Mat. "You may have a point."

Mat snorted, then mimed tipping his hat to her as he ambled off into the lunch crowd. She watched him retreat, allowing herself a few moments to finally gawk at the artistic wonder of his ass filling out his pants.

"You know it's not polite to stare," a voice said from behind her.

Luce jumped, then gave a mock growl as she spun to face her new friend Delilah.

"It's not polite to sneak up on people, and yet you do it to me almost every day."

"It's not my fault that you are extraordinarily jumpy."

"You and your ninja stealth."

"Cat-like reflexes." Delilah grinned and hopped up onto the counter. Her purple dreadlocks flowed down her back in two ponytails and she kicked her legs out, showing off multi-colored striped stockings and silver Doc Martens. "How much longer are you stuck here for?"

"Why does everybody think I'm stuck here?"

Delilah angled her head toward the candy shop she owned. "It's a mad house in there, I need a break. Wanna blow this joint and go to the Crabhouse?"

"You're going to abandon your own store? Sounds unprofessional to me."

She shrugged. "I didn't claim to be a professional, I just make candy. Besides, that's why I hired the minions."

In the mere weeks it had been in operation, Delilah's Candy Bar had become one of the most popular shops in the Button Factory. Her homemade

goodies rivaled the city's more famous candy supplier, Ghirardelli, in taste, plus she had treats no one else could think up: strawberry candy cane spun sugar, blueberry chocolate cups, mango mint licorice. Some of it sounded like it wouldn't work, but once your tongue met her candy, you were convinced she was magic.

"Sorry, I can't bail," Luce said. "Since I was covering down here, I have a ton of work to do upstairs. I'll be eating lunch at my desk today."

Delilah frowned elaborately. Her expressions in general were never limited merely to her face. Usually an elbow or ankle at least was involved. Her makeup always included an intricate design painted on her face in colored sparkles. Luce thought Delilah's ancestry was Chinese, but the woman was always vague about her origins, never speaking of her family or childhood or where she'd lived before arriving in San Francisco a couple of months earlier and opening up a fine establishment specializing in sugared goods.

Once her frown was complete, Delilah hopped off the counter, eyes bright. Her moods shifted rapidly and Luce often had a hard time keeping up.

"Okay, Luce-inda," pronouncing her full name like it was two words, as she tended to. "You go back up to your corporate prison, and I'll have a super fun lunch time without you. Good luck this afternoon. Oh, and watch your head."

With a wink and a twirl she was gone.

Luce followed Delilah's purple hair until it disappeared in the sea of patrons. A five-minute interaction with her friend was exhausting. What did she mean about watching her head? Luce shrugged it off as just another odd Delilah-ism.

She definitely should have paid more attention.

CHAPTER TWO

"Can I bug you for a second?"

Luce paused her contemplation of the ceiling tiles to turn to the doorway.

Mat stood there, phone in hand, an adorably perplexed expression on his face.

"What's up?" she asked, stifling a sigh of exasperation. He had no right to be so charming even when confused.

"Bobby sent a text asking me to go down to the storage room and dig up last year's brochures—apparently there was some kind of misprint?"

"Oh, yeah, they used the old logo, plus the telephone number was wrong. Otherwise they were perfect."

Mat smiled. It was definitely safer to focus her gaze on a spot on his shirt as opposed to being hypnotized by his perfect, even teeth.

"I'm not exactly sure where the storage room is, and Bobby's not great with specifics." He motioned toward his phone.

This time Luce smiled. Their boss was a great guy, but how he ever made it into management was a mystery. He was completely disorganized and mentally scattered—frankly, it was like working for her parents. His text had no doubt been filled with half-formed thoughts and an utter lack of coherency.

"It's in the basement, otherwise known as the crypt."

Mat's eyebrows shot up.

"Didn't you hear—that's where they keep the bodies?"

His lips twisted into a sexy smirk, and she shook her head to dislodge her wayward thoughts. "Don't worry about it, I'll take you down there. The place is kind of twisty and turny. Our storage area is almost impossible to find if you haven't been before."

She led the way to the elevator where they rode down in slightly awkward silence. On the first floor, they wound their way through the light early afternoon crowd to the stairwell leading to the horror movie set the Factory called a basement. The bottom level had not been renovated like the rest of the building and held a snarling labyrinth of corridors and hidden rooms. Needless to say, it wasn't her favorite place.

Most of the center's shops had been assigned storage rooms here, but few used them. The business office, of course, was one of the few. Their room was located at the end of a long and poorly lit hallway. Even with Mat beside her she wished she'd brought her pepper spray.

"Here we go," she said, stopping in front of an enormous metal sliding door. She grabbed the handle and began to pull. The thing had evidently been constructed to withstand a nuclear holocaust; it creaked and groaned its disapproval at being disturbed. Mat reached over her, caging her in his arms as he helped push the door along. When they'd managed it, Luce stepped back into the wall of his chest and stifled a squeak. For the life of her, she couldn't remember her checklist. She definitely wasn't breathing; she should do something about that soon. But maybe asphyxiating would be a kinder way to go. Death by daydreaming about Mat's arms wrapped around her seemed more cruel.

To make matters worse, he placed his hands on her shoulders before removing his chest from her back.

"Thanks," he said, then ducked into the room.

"No problem."

She had a new checklist now with only one thing on it: bring her heartbeat down to an acceptable level. One that would allow some of that blood to flow to the areas of her body that needed it, like her legs, so she could get the hell away from here.

"You good?" she called out.

Mat didn't respond.

"I'll just leave you to it, okay?"

Still nothing.

She stepped into the storeroom, lit only by a few bare lightbulbs in the ceiling. Two tiny, grimy windows near the ceiling obscured more sunlight than they let in. The interior was lined with imposing metal shelves overflowing with boxes of everything under the sun from cleaning supplies and ancient computer equipment to office products and coils of cables. She passed a box inexplicably filled with what looked like old typewriter keys. Ironically, there were no buttons to be found.

She waded past piles of discarded furniture, a few giant canvas bags stenciled with the word "LAUNDRY," and a stack of bicycle tires, when the floor began to move. At first it was a gentle shudder, like a semi-truck passing by, then it grew to a mighty shake.

The shelves surrounding her creaked and groaned, then began depositing their contents on the ground. A large box full of yellowed notepads clunked down on Luce's foot and she screamed.

The emptying shelf wobbled on sturdy legs and tipped toward her. Her foot was trapped, pinned under the box, and she watched in slow motion as the shelf, which definitely weighed more than she did, tilted toward her head.

Mat appeared out of nowhere and dove for her. The force of his tackle freed her foot and they fell just out of reach of the toppling shelf of death. She didn't have to remind herself to breathe this time—her lungs were gasping in as much oxygen as they could. In fact, she was in danger of hyperventilating.

Before she could even process how much of his body was in contact with hers, he rose to his knees. He wrapped an arm around her, half-crawling, half-dragging her toward the center of the room, away from the falling shelves and underneath a rusted metal desk. Luce squeezed her eyes shut and curled her body into a ball in the small space. Her foot throbbed. She shivered uncontrollably.

The rumbling stopped several hours later. Or rather several seconds later, but they were the longest of her life.

"Was that your first earthquake?" she asked once her breathing had slowed enough to allow speech.

Though her eyes were still closed, she felt a movement beside her that could have been Mat shaking his head. "I've been through a couple in Asia and one in LA a few years back. But you never really get used to them."

She nodded, or at least thought she was nodding, but for some reason her entire body was still convulsing. Goosebumps covered her bare arms. She squeezed them around her knees and tightened every muscle to stop the shaking but couldn't manage it.

Mat's arm slid around her. She leaned into him, grateful for the warmth, though it wasn't the cold that was bothering her. They sat in silence, him rubbing her arms gently until, finally, her trembling subsided.

"Thanks." She pulled away and scooted out from under the desk. Her foot was beginning to swell already. She rotated her ankle gingerly and wiggled her blue-painted toes, extraordinarily glad that she'd splurged for a pedicure the week before.

Mat slid out beside her, staring at her foot. "May I?" he asked. Before she could answer, or mentally run down the pros and cons of allowing any further skin to skin contact, his hands were on her foot, squeezing gently and tilting it back and forth.

Her ankle definitely hurt, but his hands sliding across the sensitive soles of her feet was way more stimulating than painful. Screw the checklist, she couldn't stop herself from staring at his fingers touching her. When he skimmed her arch, she

hissed in a breath, then let out a giggle. His brows rose in question.

"That tickled."

His eyes grew dark and mischievous; she could almost see him tucking that bit of information away for the future.

"I don't think it's broken," he said, pulling his hands away. A wave of relief surged through her, mixed with only the tiniest bit of disappointment.

"But maybe I should bow out of that marathon I've been training for?"

He smiled, then sat back on his haunches regarding the area. It had been a disaster zone before the earthquake; now it was post-apocalyptic. The contents of virtually every shelf had been vomited onto the ground. They sat in front of the old desk on the only spot with a clearly visible floor, an island in a sea of detritus.

The force of the quake had also slid the main door shut, but more than that, two of the heavy shelves had fallen in front of it, blocking their exit. There was no way to move the shelves. Luce wondered how they'd all gotten down here in the first place or whether the building had been built around them.

Climbing over them was a possibility, but when Mat tried, he couldn't reach the handle. Luce suspected even if he could, he wouldn't have enough leverage to wrench open the door.

He sat down next to her, covered in sweat and dust and more gorgeous than ever because of it. He pulled his cell phone from his pocket, but there were no bars, either due to their subterranean status or as a result of the lines being overloaded from the earthquake fallout. Luce's phone was upstairs at her desk.

"Looks like we're stuck," he said, putting the phone away.

Great.

CHAPTER THREE

Stuck.

In the creepy storage room.

With Mat.

There was no upside to this situation. Yes, she had delicious man-candy to stare at, but she wasn't supposed to be staring. The checklist forbade it. Not falling into a puddle at the man's feet was a top priority.

fight the system, go against the grain, and do things their own way. We lived in a van for two years. They wanted to live in a treehouse, but Child Protective Services didn't think kindly of that idea."

She didn't mention that *she* had been the one to call CPS on her own parents at the age of eleven. Somehow she didn't think Mat would sympathize. He likely would have appreciated her unconventional upbringing.

"Normal might be for suckers, but when you're a kid who's got to take care of herself from practically the time she's born, then you may wish for a little normal."

After that she couldn't think of anything else to say. So much for agreeable conversation. Luce didn't feel bad for challenging Mat's assumptions—people like him never thought any further than their own excitement or idea of happiness. Others rarely came into the equation. What Luce hated more than anything else was selfishness. She'd been surrounded by it her entire life.

Even now, as she paid most of her parents' expenses, made sure her dad took his medication and didn't miss his doctor appointments, she wondered what it would be like to not have to take care of everything. To have someone care more about her than about themselves.

She sighed, repositioning herself on the uncomfortable concrete floor. Maybe one day she'd find out. She looked over at Mat. He was so beautiful—perfect lips, perfect smile, perfect ass. Genuinely nice. Good with kids. A really decent guy. But under all of that was someone whose big picture was a little too self-centered.

She didn't think she'd need her checklist any more. Now that she knew what was beneath the surface, looking-but-not-touching would be easy.

Forty-seven hours later—or maybe ninety minutes—a jangle at the door alerted them to their rescue.

"Hello?" a muffled voice called out.

Luce stood, balancing on her good leg. Mat popped up and shouted. The massive sliding door wrenched open; behind it were Randy, another security guard, and a beaming Delilah.

Mat helped Luce climb over the toppled shelves and out into the hallway, which appeared far less

scary now that it held salvation. Luce collapsed into Delilah's open arms wanting to cry.

"There, there," Delilah said, patting her head granny style.

"Thank God!" Luce exclaimed. "I thought they were going to find our dry bones centuries from now in some sort of archeological dig."

"Dramatic much?" Delilah said. "I peeped you going down here before the seismic plates hit the fan. It just took a while to clear everything out upstairs and calm folks down. Hasn't anybody ever been through an earthquake before?" She rolled her eyes. "So," she said, drawing out the word and waggling her eyebrows suggestively in Mat's direction. He stood several feet away talking to Randy.

"Ugh, no. Not even."

Delilah executed a miniature frown. "Wait, what happened? Sweetie, if you couldn't make it work trapped in a storage room all damsel in distress-like, I don't know what to do with you."

Luce led her farther down the hall. "He and I are not compatible. Big picture, world-view type stuff. Republican-Democrat type stuff."

Delilah gasped. "He's a Republican?"

"No, I mean I don't know, doubtful, but he might as well be. He's just an overgrown child with no responsibilities and no desire for any, and I already have two sixty-year-old children. I don't need another adult to take care of."

Luce threaded her arm through Delilah's and limped toward the stairwell, eager to be out of the dungeon.

CHAPTER FOUR

"Play it again," Charlotte said, her smile set to one thousand watts.

Mat sighed and restarted the video from the beginning. He sat next to his sister in her tiny kitchen, hunched over her laptop, watching the video for the fifth time.

"It already has over ten thousand views and it's only been up two days!" Charlotte rocked back and forth with excitement.

"How many of those views are you?" Mat teased, wrapping an arm around her. He'd never seen his sister look so happy, which was say lotte's natural facial expression was a smile, but for the last two days she'd been glowing with joy. Her curly hair teetered haphazardly in a messy bun on the top of her head, and her eyes shone with delight as she showed off the impressive ring weighing down her finger.

"Micah had been planning it for weeks," she said, sparkling just as brightly as her diamond. "Almost since we first met."

On the video, Micah, Charlotte's musician boyfriend of one year, sat on a bicycle with a guitar, strumming while pedaling with no hands. He sang a very silly song about Charlotte and how much he loved her, rhyming her name with "harlot," "varmint," and "marmoset."

As he wound his way through Golden Gate park, costumed dancers popped out from behind trees singing verses and performing choreographed steps. At the song's finale, several dozen people crowded the screen singing and dancing in unison. Micah stopped the bike and remained balanced as he sang the last verse, rhyming "verily" with "marry me." The camera panned around to reveal a very teary Charlotte sitting on a golf cart, watching the show firsthand. Micah got on one knee and placed the two-carat diamond on her slender finger.

"Seriously, though. I'm impressed. Micah's a great guy. With a lot of crazy friends." Mat reached for his mug of coffee next to the computer.

Charlotte admired her ring, her eyes a little wistful. "Yeah, he's amazing. Of course I haven't said yes yet."

Mat choked, nearly spitting the coffee onto the computer. "What? Why not? I thought you were madly in love."

"I am, of course I am. I can't imagine being with anyone else."

"So what is it?"

"You know he'll be on tour half of the year. Europe then Asia."

Micah was the drummer for the band RiotSphere, who'd had a track go viral the year before. When Charlotte met him, he'd been back home in Hill Valley, considering leaving the group. But after the lead singer left to go solo, Micah's other bandmates had begged him to return. They'd been in the studio for the past few months recording their next album with Charlotte helping to pen some of the tracks.

"I just don't think a long-distance relationship can work. I mean, look what happened with Mom and Dad, right?"

"Well, why don't you go with him?" Mat asked. "I don't get it. Is it your job?"

"No, my boss is fine with me being a virtual assistant. And I can work on my screenplay from anywhere, I just…." She twisted the ring on her finger once, then turned her gaze to him. She looked so much like their mother with her blonde hair and green eyes, it still sometimes startled him. Her skin was golden brown, so light it could pass for a perpetual tan, and many people didn't realize she was half-black.

Mat was a few shades darker, but knew well the stigma of being thought as "not black enough." He'd gotten the sense that the feeling of not being accepted, or being sought after for the wrong reasons, had seeped into Charlotte's relationships. Her ex had cheated on her with one of her close friends, so Mat was glad she'd found Micah. He was a really good guy and great for Charlotte. So her reluctance to accept his proposal just didn't make sense.

"Just tell me, Char," he prompted.

"I don't know if I can just abandon you." She suddenly looked so much younger than thirty-four, but the heaviness in her eyes was old.

"What do you mean, abandon me? I'm hardly ever in one place for long anyway. I can always visit you wherever you are."

Charlotte stopped fidgeting with her ring, and her expression turned serious. He knew that look all too well—she wanted to talk about "his future."

"I'm worried about you," she said as he groaned internally. "One day, hopefully soon, you're going to want to stop being a nomad and settle down somewhere. There can't be too many places you haven't been yet, right?"

Mat snorted. "The world is a big place, Char."

"I know, I know, and traveling has its merits, but it's important to have a home base somewhere—to be settled. I just don't know how I can run off on tour with a rock band and leave you with nowhere to come home to."

Mat stilled, regarding his sister through fresh eyes. "Is that why you've stayed here in the Bay Area so long? To give me a place to come back to?" Charlotte's averted eyes gave him his answer.

"Char, I never wanted you to put anything on hold for me—especially not getting married. I'm a grown-up and I love you and appreciate your concern, but I'm not your responsibility anymore."

"You're my brother and I love you and want you to be happy. I've been taking care of you forever. I don't really know how to stop." Her sad smile broke his heart, especially since he was the reason for erasing the joy from a few minutes before.

"I can't help worrying. You don't have any close friends, no girlfriend, just temporary, freelance design gigs for income. It's always been the two of us, we've always depended on each other. With Dad being—" she waved her hand in the air, "—the way he is, and Mom and her shiny new family, how could I live with myself if I left you too? Everybody needs somewhere to come home to."

She shook her head when Mat tried to speak. "I know you think I'm a crazy worry-wart. I don't need a lecture on the convenience of modern travel." Her eyes teared up. "And I know you're not the same little kid who fell apart when Mom left. But ever since that day I've made sure you had a home. You might not think you need it, but I know you do. I know how you look when you get off a plane from God knows where, and I see the change that happens while you're here. A part of that little boy is still inside of you, and I promised him I'd never abandon him. No matter what."

Her face was wet as she pulled him into an embrace. "It would be different if you had someone," she whispered into his neck.

Mat couldn't stand seeing Charlotte cry. He hated the guilt that gnawed at him, threatening to tear him open from the inside out. He did owe her. When their mom left, their dad had been deployed. What started as a weekend trip back home to Norway kept being extended longer and longer. She would call and promise she was coming back in a few days, and then never show up.

They had been convinced their father didn't know. He never mentioned anything in their infrequent phone calls, and since she claimed to be coming back, they never said anything. After a few weeks, her phone calls stopped. Calls to their grandparents' house in Oslo went unanswered. Messages unreturned.

Ten-year-old Mat began failing classes, getting into fights, stealing. He grew more withdrawn until he was just a ball of anger looking for an outlet. When their dad finally returned home, Mat had assumed they would pick up the broken pieces of their family and put them back together in a new formation. A puzzle, slightly skewed, some of the parts in the wrong place, but still something.

But their dad poured himself into his job. They moved again, and then again, as he sought higher rank. Within a year, Mat was lucky if he saw his father once a week. It was Charlotte who'd calm his sudden rages. She studied child psychology books and pelted him with art supplies until he finally began to draw and found a way to manage his emotions.

She signed the permission slips, made dinner, helped with his homework. Came to his art shows and basketball games. She'd postponed college until he graduated from high school and was probably the only reason he'd finished school at all.

And he'd thanked her by taking off the first chance he could, never realizing she was still putting her life on hold so he'd always have a place to retreat to.

Overgrown child. Another adult to take care of. He'd overheard Luce talking with Delilah after their rescue the other day. The words stung. He hadn't meant to antagonize her. Even now, the soft fruit and cocoa butter scent surrounding her licked at his senses.

He'd noticed her velvety, dark chocolate skin and full, sensual lips the first day he started work, though unlike some of the other women there, she was not in obvious pursuit of him. That was for the best—he'd learned not to shit where he ate. Workplace romances got complicated, and he avoided complicated at all costs.

Anything more than a brief fling was off-limits. He'd tried the girlfriend thing. Dated a graduate student in Italy for close to three months. When it was time for him to go, he'd even asked her to come with him. But she had roots, a family, a thesis to finish. Sure, he could have stayed, but then what? Eventually, something would happen to tear them apart. *Der gror ikke mose på rullande stein.* A rolling stone gathers no moss. He learned that from his mother.

The only one he'd ever counted on was Charlotte. She loved him unconditionally, and would continue to put her life on hold while he figured out his.

If he let that happen, he deserved to be chewed apart by the gnawing jaws of guilt. He would deserve so much worse.

When she was with Micah, it was like she was the person she was always meant to be. He had to figure out how to convince her that he would be all right.

It would be different if you had someone.

Mat squeezed his sister. "Listen." His mind raced, traveling a little slower than his mouth. "I wasn't gonna tell you until I was—until we—but, well, there's this girl…"

Charlotte let out a squeak and pulled back, wiping her nose and eyes. "Who is she? Why am I just hearing about this? When do I get to meet her?"

"Well—we've only been out a few times, so I didn't want to jinx it by telling you about her, but she's pretty amazing. I think it might be serious."

"Where did you meet her? At work?" Charlotte asked, her smile erasing all traces of tears.

"Yeah." Mat nodded, pushing aside the murmurings of his conscience.

"What's her name?" Charlotte asked.

Her name.

Mat replied with the only name he could think of, regretting it as soon as the word passed his lips. "Luce, her name is Luce."

Charlotte was glowing again. "Luce. I like her already."

CHAPTER FIVE

Luce walked back to her office from the copy room, arms laden with the collated and stapled budget packets she'd spent the last forty-five minutes putting together. Weren't there interns who did this kind of thing? She stopped just in front of her door as an unfamiliar woman approached.

"Can I help you?" she asked.

The woman smiled, and Luce instantly liked her. She was gorgeous, but with her simple, slouchy clothes and messy bun, you could tell she didn't pay much attention to her appearance.

"I'm looking for Lucinda Garvey."

"That's me."

"Luce!" The woman's smile grew impossibly larger, like she'd just met her oldest friend after years apart.

"Um, hi." Luce motioned to her office and set her papers down on her desk. As soon as her arms were clear, the woman pulled her into a huge bear hug. Her tiny arms were surprisingly strong.

On the other hand, maybe the woman's appearance was less "I don't care" and more "I'm crazy."

Luce pulled back. "Um—have we met?"

The woman laughed. "Sorry, I'm Charlotte. I was just so excited I couldn't wait to meet you. I know I shouldn't bug you at work."

Luce kept smiling, racking her brain for knowledge of anyone called Charlotte. This woman couldn't be crazy—no mentally ill people sported ice like the one weighing down Charlotte's ring finger, right? She decided to play along, hoping she hadn't forgotten anyone important.

"Sit down, please."

"So you're coming this weekend?" Charlotte asked.

Luce took a deep breath and realized she wasn't going to be able to play along after all. "I'm sorry, what's happening this weekend?"

Charlotte's face morphed to shock. "Mat didn't tell you?"

Mat. Didn't he mention a sister called Charlotte? There was some resemblance now that she looked harder.

"I haven't seen Mat yet today."

"Oh," Charlotte's smile returned. "Let me send you the invite. Once I finally said yes to Micah, he found out the record company had scheduled a couple of tour dates in the U.S. The first one's in Vegas, so we're actually getting married in two weeks!" She jumped up and down. "Anyway, the ceremony is going to be really tiny, so Micah's mother is insisting we have this blowout engagement party with our family and friends *this* weekend in Napa. She rented out an entire vineyard for it and everything." She took a deep breath. "So what's your email?"

Luce was going to have to put crazy back on the table as a possibility, but Charlotte was so nice, so friendly, so amazingly excited, that Luce didn't want to burst the bubble she was living in. And it's not like her email address was a social security number. How much damage could the woman do?

Still, something weird was going on and she wanted to get to the bottom of it. After Charlotte finished typing, Luce said, "You know, why don't we go see Mat right now? You can't stop by without visiting him, right?"

"Of course not. He's not too busy, do you think?"

"Too busy for his sister?"

They rose and made their way down the hall to the cubicle where Mat sat, his back to them, headphones on. Charlotte snuck up behind him and covered his eyes with her hands. He spun around, pulling off his headphones, then froze when he saw Luce standing behind his sister.

"Hey," he said looking back and forth between the two women.

"Look who I found in the hallway," Luce said in a sing-song voice, crossing her arms. "And why am I just hearing about this whole Napa thing now?" She put a note of playful censure into her voice, but her eyes bored holes into Mat.

He stood, hugged his sister then moved to stand awkwardly beside Luce.

"Can I get a picture of you guys?" Charlotte asked, giddy. "I've never had one of Mat and his girlfriend."

Mat turned to stone beside her, and Luce kept her face neutral, only by virtue of the fact that she had so many years of practice dealing with unexplained occurrences caused by her parents.

"By all means, take a picture of Mat with his girlfriend. Can I be in it too?"

"Oh, I like her," Charlotte said, laughing, and raised her phone. "Closer you guys."

Mat slid closer and put an arm around Luce. His smile was tight as the shutter sound clicked.

"I'm going to let you guys get back to work. It was so wonderful meeting you, Luce!"

Charlotte pulled Luce in for another massive hug.

"You too." Despite the fact that she was going to murder her brother in short order, Luce really did like Charlotte.

"I'll see you next weekend."

Luce smiled and nodded, but didn't respond. With a hug and a kiss for Mat, Charlotte was gone in a whirlwind of strawberry shampoo.

Luce turned on Mat just as the receptionist, Mina, sauntered down the hallway, swaying her hips seductively and pulling down the hem of her V neck sweater to expose more of her cleavage. Luce rolled her eyes.

"Hi, Mat," she said, actually batting her eyelashes.

Mat nodded tightly, barely looking at her.

"Um, I was wondering if you could help me with something. It's a Photoshop thing, and I know you're the expert."

Mina was shameless. It's like she had her own clichéd flirting checklist. Toss hair, check. Bite lip, check. Luce waited for her to run her hand over her breasts to complete the ridiculousness.

"Hi, Mina," Luce said. The younger woman finally noticed Luce and waved in her direction.

"So, Mat, whenever, you know, you get a chance," Mina said.

"Sure, I'll come by later."

"Thanks, so much!" She sauntered closer and ran her hand down his biceps. Then she spun, her flared skirt twirling up almost revealing her underwear—if she was wearing any. If she sashayed any harder walking away she would probably sprain something.

"Oh, Luce," she called over her shoulder. "Bobby wanted me to tell you the budget meeting's in five minutes."

Luce rolled her eyes, then turned back to Mat. She pointed her finger at him, but the words wouldn't come. "I don't even have time for this right now."

He started to speak but she cut him off. "After work. The Candy Bar."

He closed his mouth and nodded. She shook her head and went back to her office.

As she stacked the budget reports and put them in manila folders, one thought circled her mind over and over. Why did Mat involve *her* in his little scheme—whatever it was?

Delilah's Candy Bar was set up like an actual bar, with bartenders serving candy cocktails and assorted treats. There was a self-service section on the opposite wall where customers could fill bags full of sweets and pay by the pound.

Luce sat at the bar, sipping a delicious white chocolate virgin martini. The concoction was normally a guaranteed pick me up, but it wasn't doing the trick this evening.

She felt Mat's arrival, could tell he was looking at her based on how she suddenly felt flushed, her skin too hot and tight. She swiveled on the bar stool to monitor his approach—slow, as if he was nearing a wild animal. He sat next to her.

Luce waited for him to say something. She refused to be the one to break the silence.

"I'm really sorry," he said, finally. "This whole thing got kinda out of hand."

"You think?"

Some of her icy anger melted at the sincerity in his expression. Like a faucet opening, he poured out the story of Charlotte's impending marriage and how she would only say yes if she felt that he was settled. His mouth had gotten him into trouble, and he'd said Luce's name in a fit of desperation. He hadn't been prepared for how very much Charlotte would want to meet her.

"My sister, she practically raised me. She's given up a lot for me and I just…I wanted to reassure her. I'm really sorry."

Luce gripped onto her empty martini glass. "I just don't understand…. Why me?"

He turned to her, a curious expression on his face.

"I mean, I'm sure Mina would do a great job being your pretend girlfriend. Or Farrah. I'm sure either one of them would be—very thorough." Luce pushed away the image that threatened to surface.

Mat frowned. "I don't really know why. Your name was just the first to come into my head."

Luce sat back in her seat. There was no wacky romantic comedy setup; he didn't secretly have feelings for her. He literally just said the first name that popped into his head. What did she expect?

"Charlotte really likes you."

She turned to him, incredulous. "She's pretty awesome, but there's no way I can pretend to be your girlfriend for an entire weekend. You get that, right?"

"Yeah, sure. Of course." He sat back. "It's just she really likes you. She texted me that she thinks you're a good influence on me."

"So I'll be your mentor. Train you in the ways of responsible human behavior. Teach you to use the Force. But your girlfriend? Mat, seriously."

"Do you want money?"

She guffawed. "You're trying to buy me? Why don't you go find a call girl? Tell Charlotte that we broke up but you've found a new love of your life." She stood in a huff.

"Luce, wait, I didn't mean it like that." He reached out and held her elbow—his touch was like an anchor weighing her feet to the ground. "Is there

anything that would make you agree to this? I know it's asking a lot."

She wrenched free of his grip, her skin tingling from the lost contact. She couldn't look at him. She wanted to help, and couldn't bear the thought of someone as sweet as Charlotte missing out on the love of her life, as improbable as it was—but this really wasn't going to work.

"I'm really sorry, Mat. I want to be able to help, I just can't. I think you need to tell your sister the truth."

He nodded slowly, rising. "No, I understand. I shouldn't have gotten you involved. *I'm* sorry."

With a final look he turned and left the store.

"How do I get into these situations?" Luce said, dropping her head into her hands. "Is this officially a fiasco?"

The jingling of bells announced Delilah's arrival across the bar. "I think it would need to be way wackier to reach fiasco territory. It sounds like he was in a bind."

Luce looked up. "A bind? And now I'm expected to take part in some kind of romantic comedy premise? It's insane. I think the sanity of that entire family should be called into question." Luce shook her head. "Do you really think she'll call off the wedding if she finds out Mat doesn't have a girlfriend?"

"You did say she was crazy."

Luce drained her sugartini and shook her head. "It doesn't make any sense."

"Would you take off on a world tour and leave your parents to fend for themselves? If your dad wasn't sick, but they were still…"

"Emotional infants? Unable to manage even the remote semblance of a normal adult thought process?" Luce's shoulders sagged. "But Mat is functional."

"Your parents have managed to keep themselves alive for sixty years."

"Barely," Luce muttered.

"Besides, didn't you always want a life full of adventure?"

Luce stared at her. "No. I wanted a life full of normalcy. Regular school. Bedtimes. Running water. I've had quite enough adventure."

Delilah stared meaningfully at Luce. "PR normal? Budget report normal? Don't you miss the drama just a teeny, tiny bit?"

Luce was unwilling to admit any truth to Delilah's assertions. Yes, her job was just the teensiest bit boring, and yes she missed the hustle and bustle of being in the thick of things at the info desk downstairs. She'd even thought it might be nice to work for one of the tour companies, leading visitors around the city she'd claimed as her own after her parents had finally settled in one place.

Luce shook her head. "It's too much. Besides, all that deception just doesn't sit right with me." She tapped her fingers on the bar before rising to leave. The last thing she needed was another fiasco.

CHAPTER SIX

Luce dropped her keys on the entry table in her parents' hallway and slumped against the wall. The smell of smoke filled the apartment.

"Joyce!" The apartment was cluttered, as usual. It was saved from official hoarder status because of Luce's careful ministrations. She waded through, picking up trash, pushing shoes and cartons out of the way until she reached the bedroom in the back.

Her father, Moses, sat in his wheelchair next to the open window, hastily stubbing out a cigarette. Joyce sat next to him, looking guilty.

Luce sighed. "Didn't the doctor tell you just this last week? No. More. Cigarettes."

She grabbed the package on the window sill, a new one since she'd just done a sweep the day before, and stuffed it in her pocket.

"And you!" she turned to her mother.

Joyce looked away sheepishly.

"I've already got the damn 'zema," Moses said. "So why can't I keep smoking?"

Luce stalked over and picked up her father's oxygen mask, handing it to him. He grumbled as he stuck the tubes into his nose. "This doggone thing is uncomfortable as hell."

"Good," she said, picking up the ashtray and dumping it into the trash.

"Mom, you can't keep buying him cigarettes. This has to stop. Did you listen to anything the doctor said?"

"The doctor said he was getting worse," her mother chirped. "There's no cure for COPD, so he may as well smoke while he's still here."

"Do you even want to still be here?" She rounded on her father.

He sat there wheezing, his eyes watering. A round of coughing was about to start. She moved the box of tissues closer to him so he could catch the blood and mucus his lungs were spewing out. She didn't want to watch though.

As she left the room, her mother spoke loudly over her father's coughing fit. "I'll never understand why that gal takes things so seriously. She could suck the fun out of anything."

Luce headed to the kitchen to make sure there was food in the fridge. She found a few cartons of takeout that smelled relatively edible.

"I'm leaving!" she called, sticking her head back through the bedroom doorway.

"Good riddance!" her father said, turning away to stare out the window. Her mother shrugged her shoulders as if to say, *You know how your father is.* Absolving herself of any responsibility. As usual.

Luce locked their door and trudged up the stairs to her apartment. But before she'd made it a few steps, her mother's voice rose behind her.

"I forgot to tell you. The landlord called and said that he was finally going to fumigate our apartment this weekend. Dad and I will need to stay with you for a couple of days."

Luce's knuckles cracked. She looked down to find that her fists were clenched so tightly she was in danger of losing feeling in her fingers.

"Why does your apartment need to be fumigated?" Her jaw ached from the tension of forcing the words through closed teeth.

Her mother twisted one of the rings that decorated each of her fingers. "I may have found a pizza box that I'd forgotten about."

"Found it where?"

"Possibly under the bed." Her mother's eyes darted around. "And covered in roaches."

Luce felt a gush of air escape from her body.

"It'sjustacoupleofdays. It'llbelikeoldtimes." Joyce's words rushed together in one big jumble and then she was gone. Slamming the door before Luce could even respond.

Luce shut her eyes and counted to ten. She'd lived here since her last year of college, the top floor of an adorable duplex. Once her father's COPD had gotten severe and her parents had been kicked out of yet another apartment, Luce had talked to her landlord and arranged to have her parents move in downstairs when the old tenant left.

Taking care of them was almost a full-time job, and most days, she didn't know why she bothered. They were never grateful, they never saw her as a loving daughter, just a nagging inconvenience out to spoil their carefree lifestyle. Though how carefree they could be in the face of her father's debilitating illness was unknown.

She paid their rent, made sure they had enough food, took her dad to the doctor, and made sure he took his medicine. She tried to keep him from smoking and doing the other things that would exacerbate his condition. And for all that, she got nothing in return. Not even an *I love you*.

Once inside her own apartment, she sank onto her couch and toed off her shoes. Her ankle was still sore, but the swelling had gone down and she could walk without a problem. She rubbed the joint until the acheyness abated. The last thing she needed was an injury.

A boyfriend, on the other hand, would be nice. A real one, not the acting challenge that Mat offered. Someone to rub her hurt ankle. Ask about her day. She sighed, leaning back.

She'd always sought out the most normal, stable men she could find. Accountants. Law students. Insurance guys. The only problem with these guys was they didn't have much to talk about outside of work, sports, and television. Luce knew that if she kept at it she could find someone both interesting and reliable. When she did, she wouldn't let him go.

As a lonely kid, she'd been shuffled around while her father tried his best to make a living without actually having a job. Before she was born, he'd been a poet and taught college-level poetry, which was where he'd met her mother, who'd been going back to school after years away. Even though the age difference wasn't significant, the university frowned on professor-student relationships and he was fired. After that, the two of them decided that the system was for suckers.

They traveled the country. Sometimes he'd pick up an adjunct professor gig for a semester or two,

but inevitably there was some reason why that particular institution was not right for him.

He'd made a name for himself in the seventies with his black-power poetry, and had been paid to speak and lecture. He also wrote manifestos and editorial think pieces on a range of social topics.

Her mother had dropped out of college the first time to model. After meeting Moses and dropping out again, she just followed wherever he went. Her official job, Luce always thought, was hype-woman. You know how rappers always have someone else on stage with them hyping up the crowd, getting them to throw their hands in the air and shout and all that? That was Joyce's specialty. She served as barker for his public lectures, enticing folks to come up and hear him speak. At poetry readings, she was always engaging the crowd. She was good with people—that's where Luce got it from—but her work ethic beyond her husband's career was nil.

The thought of the two of them infecting the peace Luce had painstakingly created in her home with all of their noise and smoke and messiness—*roaches? Seriously?*—was not something she was ready to even consider.

If the two of them were going to invade her apartment for an entire weekend, then Luce needed to be far, far away.

Like Napa? She shushed the little voice inside her head. It was evil and traitorous and…and…just plain mean. Besides, Napa wasn't even that far away. And Luce wasn't a wine drinker. She hated the heady, briny smell of the stuff. She barely liked grapes when they weren't fermented—what would she do in Napa for an entire weekend?

Have a free vacation. Relax. Be away from Moses and Joyce. Would those two be able to survive for two days without her? She sniffed.

Maybe she could convince Delilah to come and look in on them at least once.

Besides, there were other things to do in Napa besides drink wine. And Charlotte was so sweet. Letting her live under the delusion that her brother was getting himself together and turning into a responsible person in a real relationship wasn't the worst thing in the world. Anything for love, right?

The idea of spending a weekend with Mat was daunting, but Luce had faced tougher obstacles in life. She'd worked her way through college and was well on her way to being the master of her own destiny.

She grabbed her phone and pulled up the company phone list.

So what if her greatest acting accomplishment thus far was playing a tree in her sixth-grade play? She'd made one awesome tree. Pretending to be Mat's girlfriend couldn't be that much harder, could it?

Our columnist, Julie Pitzel, has been a receptionist, radio DJ, bill collector, telemarketer, administrative assistant, community college instructor, and an expediter (aka professional nag). She's been involved in the Houston writing community for many years, including two years as president of a local Romance Writers of America Chapter. She writes paranormal fiction from a geodesic dome south of Houston, where she lives with her husband and a pair of cats. Most recently, her story "The Dance" was published in The Death of All Things *anthology.*

I'LL CRY IF I WANT TO

by Julie Pitzel

I read a wide variety of genres, from romance to mystery to science fiction. I read funny stories and dark tales with warped twists. When hunting for books, I look for words like fast-paced, humorous, thrilling, chilling, and adventurous. The words I avoid are poignant, emotional, moving, and especially heart-rending. Those descriptions indicate the story will be sad and I'll cry. I don't want to cry. At this time of my life, I'd much rather laugh or experience the excitement—even the terror—from a tense adventure than ugly-cry over fictional people. But that hasn't always been the case. There are times I think all of us want and need the cathartic release of blubbering over characters we know only from the pages of a good novel.

I usually try to avoid the blurry vision, blotchy face, and runny nose, but I know plenty of people who enjoy a good cry. And according to *Medical News Today*, there are several benefits to tearing up. Their studies show that the emotional release can have a self-soothing effect by activating the parasympathetic nervous system which helps us relax. Surprisingly, crying can release endorphins and other "feel good" chemicals which actually improve our mood. Those same chemicals can relieve emotional and some physical pain. Researchers found that some tears contain stress hormones, and so by crying we may be shedding toxins and stress. And by reducing stress and pain, it could also be a sleep aid. Obviously crying all of the time isn't good, but giving in to the occasional cryfest is normal and healthy.

Part of the reason I avoid sad tales is because I cry so very easily. Commercials about puppies and heart-warming memes about heroes have me sniffling and rubbing my eyes. But even if I avoid the ten-hanky movies, many books and shows sneak in scenes that make me cry. Some even manage to make me cry and laugh at the same time. The movie *Up* had that opening that could make the hardest heart weep, and then go back and watch it again. We don't expect to sob at a Star Trek movie, but when Spock dies in *Wrath of Khan*, it's difficult to remain dry eyed. Too many romances have me pulling out the tissues when the couple finally figures out they belong together. I often read at the gym, the lunchroom at work, or other public places, and it can be awkward explaining to a coworker that I'm fine as tears streak my cheeks.

And when I do want that emotional release, what better reason to cry than a good romance? Most romances deal with emotionally—and sometimes physically—damaged characters who learn to deal with their damage while falling in love with another injured soul. There are stories of veterans struggling with PTSD, parents recovering from the loss of a child, or victims of rape or abuse putting one foot in front of the other. These are characters just trying to get through one more day and suddenly they're introduced to another person who's fighting their own demons but who helps make the daily struggle just a little bit easier. Someone comes into their life who not only accepts the damage but embraces it along with the rest of their flaws. We can read these novels or watch these movies and cry in sympathy when the bad things happen. And then produce joyful tears when we get to the happily ever after. The great thing about a tear-jerking romance is the knowledge that no matter what horrible thing happens to the characters, we know it's going to work out in the end. Broken hearts will be mended, and true love will make things better.

Different types of stories make us cry for different reasons. Beware of books and movies labeled as romantic or love stories. With a romance, no matter how poignant and tear-jerking, we know the couple will make it work out. They'll overcome all of the obstacles for a happily ever after. But a love story tricks us; it acts like a romance throwing up roadblocks and making the characters iron out their differences. Then just as we start to believe they are going to live their wonderful life together, a stupid logging truck runs over Meg Ryan. Love stories don't carry the same promise of a happily ever after as a romance, and they frequently open our tear ducts soon after we crack the spine. These are the Nicolas Sparks tales, the accounts of terminally ill or critically injured characters contemplating life and love and whether they want to continue participating in either—there's even a subgenre of YA labeled sick-lit dealing with all manner of illnesses and disabilities and heartbreak. These are the moving narratives of star-crossed lovers who enjoy two minutes of bliss only to be torn apart by war or family or their own stubborn decision to do what's right. (And yes, we agree that Ilsa should fly off with Victor Laszlo, but dammit, we also want her to stay with Rick.) If you want to ride an emotional roller coaster—and clear your sinuses—stock up on Kleenex and dive into one of these tear-jerkers.

Romances and other love stories make it safe to cry. We can let ourselves go dealing with fictional lives and loves. No matter how many tissues we use or how red our eyes get, we can be comfortable indulging because we know it's a story. When we turn that final page or the credits begin to scroll, we can take a deep breath and return to our regular lives. Deeply emotional stories do stick with us, but we choose to watch or read those stories—or not. Sometimes it's comforting to see characters confront the same issues we're dealing with, whether that's divorce or terminal illness. It can help us see that we aren't alone. The book can even help us open communications with others going through the same ordeal. However, there are times when we are too vulnerable, when real life has us crying enough without any fictional help, when we're already living the experience and need to get away. If a story becomes too intense or the plot parallels our lives too closely, it's okay to close the book or turn off the movie. There are benefits to crying, but there can be too much of a good thing.

I *can* cry if I want to, but I may decide to follow up a sob-fest with a slapstick comedy.

https://www.medicalnewstoday.com/articles/319631.php

C.S. DeAvilla writes award-winning science fiction, fantasy, and romance under another pen name. She has been a romance fan since she sneaked a peek at her mother's massive historical romance bookcase and fell in love with all the characters. She reads every romance genre—as long as two people are falling in love, she'll give it a read. Her favorite authors are Jennifer Crusie, J.R. Ward, Darynda Jones, Suzanne Brockmann, Sarah MacLean, and Kristan Higgins. But she always has room for one more.

RECOMMENDED BOOKS

by C.S. DeAvilla

MADDIE DAWSON

Title: ***Matchmaking for Beginners***
Author: Maddie Dawson
Publisher: Lake Union Publishing
ASIN: B076CJX3YN
Release Date: June 1, 2018

Matchmaking for Beginners was one of those books I would have never picked up had it not been recommended to me through my retailer's recommendation engine. Well, the computers must know me pretty well because this was a joyful, unexpected surprise. *Matchmaking for Beginners* has gathered thousands of reviews in a short amount of time and for a good reason. The book is fantastic, reaching into the basic recipe of what makes a classic romance and playing with the ingredients. Marnie is ready for her life to begin—newly engaged and counting

how many kids she'll have one day in her average-sized home. Except she meets her fiancé's aunt, Blix Holliday, and her plans are thwarted by fate. Marnie isn't meant to marry Blix's nephew, but someone else, and Blix frets over how to make this happen without ruining Marnie's dream for herself. As chance would have it, Blix doesn't have to lift a finger, as her nephew leaves Marnie for Africa with a friend on a grand adventure. Marnie, however, enters her own adventure when Blix leaves her a New York townhouse after she dies. Marnie's true love lives in the basement of the complex, but Patrick won't even meet Marnie due to extensive facial scars from a fire years before. The story explores loss and grief through a new lens and when readers come out the other side of this tale it feels like a long, satisfying journey. I didn't want *Matchmaking for Beginners* to end and neither will you. It's simply fantastic.

Title: ***The Chase***
Author: Elle Kennedy
Publisher: Elle Kennedy Inc.
ASIN: B07G6M9HDV
Release Date: August 4, 2018

A few years back I became helplessly addicted to the New Adult genre in general and Elle Kennedy's Briar University hockey romance series in particular. I'm a sucker for a group of guys who interact more like family than teammates. So when I saw Kennedy had a few more books coming out that would continue the series, I squealed and marked my calendar for the newest release. Summer is the little sister to Dean, a hero from one of the earlier books set at the same university. Though the two siblings are from a well-off family, they aren't the typical rich kids, and are more down-to-Earth and realistic with their goals. So even though I normally don't connect with wealthy love interests as characters, Kennedy does a great job in character development in *The Chase*. Fritzy (Colin Fitzgerald) is a programming whiz, artist, and jock. He's fought the dumb jock stereotype his whole life and now a billionaire tech genius has his eye on him for a potential job. Aside from fighting through stereotype barriers in the geek world, he's passing the same kind of judgement on Summer DeLaurentis. She's beautiful and wild. Never had to work hard for anything. Surface level. Or so it seems. Summer does work hard, extremely hard, considering she's constantly battling her attention deficit disorder to keep her grades high and not get kicked out of Briar like she did Brown last semester. Summer and Fritz end up as roommates and the misunderstandings continue to explode and cause friction and conflicts. But that's not all. Their close proximity leads to other kinds of friction and chemistry. This is an addicting story that readers will love to add to their pile and put Elle on their auto-buy list.

Title: ***Intermediate Thermodynamics: A Romantic Comedy***
Author: Susannah Nix
Publisher: Haver Street Press
ASIN: B074HLQHPP
Release Date: October 4, 2017

One of my greatest loves is a smart heroine, and Susannah Nix takes this love to another level. Female characters in the STEM field star in her romantic comedy series and my reader heart is happy. Ester Abbot is an aerospace engineer and more than happy to continue her life with a string of relationships that lack any emotional depth, which is why her nothing-but-emotional neighbor Jonathan annoys her so much. As he finds out she has an engineering degree, he begs her to critique his science fiction script for his graduate screenwriting class. She forces him to date her best friend in return to keep her friend from slipping back into a relationship with a dude Ester believes is emotionally abusive. None of Ester's plans work out the way she's carefully set them up and it all comes tumbling down messier than a house of cards. This is the second book I've read in Nix's Chemistry Lessons romantic comedy series and each book gets better and better. Nix explores the layers and emotional depth of her characters and doesn't settle for tired clichés, making this series much more interesting when readers can never guess how the happily ever after is going to go down.

Title: ***My Favorite Half-Night Night Stand***
Author: Christina Lauren
Publisher: Gallery Books (Simon and Schuster)
ASIN: B07CLFYBCT
Release Date: December 4, 2018

One of the most difficult romances to write is the one where the couple readers are *supposed* to root for sleep together early on in the novel. It's hard to build up anticipation when the deed we're all waiting for is done on page two. But for Christina Lauren, writing team extraordinaire, I should have known this was an empty worry. Millie Morris, criminal justice professor, has a really comfortable friendship with her colleagues in the science department, especially Reid Campbell. Reid is, by far, the guy in the group she confides in more than she has any other man in her life. However, the small amount she shares isn't nearly enough for the emotionally intelligent biology professor, Reid. He craves more. One night after a little too much to drink, Millie decides to engage in casual sex with her friend Reid, an activity he's fully on board for, leaving a mere few hours later. It's all great for both of them, and they're able to continue on with very few awkward moments between them. But now that they've complicated their friendship they decide it's best not to be each other's date for the Obama speech scheduled at their college in a few weeks. The group of friends (not knowing two of their fivesome got it on) decide to join a dating site to wrangle up their dates. Millie writes their profiles, they write Millie's, but Millie decides to make her account less obvious after she's inundated with jerks and dick-pics. She's amused when the dating site matches her highly with Reid and she starts talking to him and they hit it off online. Millie, or "Catherine," opens up to Reid and he quickly falls for both of them—Millie in real life, and the emotionally more available "Catherine" online. One problem: it becomes clear that Reid has zero idea that "Catherine" is Millie no matter how much she hints at it. Christina Lauren is an auto buy for me, and this book keeps them high on that list of special authors that continue to deliver the very best in romance.

Title: ***The Tattooist of Auschwitz***
Author: Heather Morris
Publisher: HarperCollins
ASIN: B0756DZ4C1
Release Date: September 4, 2018

Drawn to the title of this romance and my interest in World War II history, I knew I had to read it. Morris sets up an inspirational love story in the midst of a grim backdrop. Concentration camps during Nazi rule were a particularly dark time in the war and the fallout continues to affect us today. Taken from a true story of detailed interviews with the person the main character is based on, readers will not be disappointed. Lale is tasked with tattooing his fellow holocaust prisoners. Wracked with guilt for his part in some way helping the Nazis, he chooses to risk his life and use his position to sneak goods and services to other prisoners. He soon meets Gita and the pair quickly fall for each other. The years that follow are a fight to stay alive and that fear doesn't end with liberation for this couple. This book will take readers to a terrible time in history, show the lowest points of how ugly hatred or indifference can destroy humanity, but also will build readers up and fill them with hope for the future. Lale and Gita remind us to never forget that love will always be stronger.

Andrea attended The Culinary Institute of America in Hyde Park, New York to study Culinary Arts in 1998. Upon graduation, she continued on at Johnson & Wales University in Providence, RI to study Food Service Management. After a few years of getting hands-on experience, Andrea was drawn to Chicago to the famed Charlie Trotters Restaurant. There, Andrea was exposed to one-of-a-kind wine cellar in which she received one of the best wine educations in the world, tasting & serving some to the most rare and most special wines ever produced. She worked with some of the world's top ingredients, Chef's, Farmers, food lover's and wine aficionados, but homesick, Andrea returned to Santa Fe, NM, where she was Partner & Head Chef at Rasa Juice Bar & Ayurveda. Andrea received many rave reviews and won the Local Hero Award 2 years in a row for her organic, plant-based café. Her attention to detail to her beautifully plated and delicious food is enhanced with the love and care she infuses into every bite! She is currently the Owner and Chef of The Temptress Private Chef & Catering operated out of her home town of Santa Fe, NM.

THE TEMPTRESS PRESENTS: CHOCOLATE BARS

Raw, Vegan & Gluten Free

by Andrea Abedi

The Temptress is excited to wish a Happy Valentine's Day to all of you lovers out there. Chocolate is magical and has the power of an aphrodisiac that lies in its micronutrients. Tryptophan (a building block of serotonin), and phenylethylamine (a part of amphetamine), are both associated with feelings of falling in love. What a perfect way to show your lover how much they mean to you than with chocolate! These chocolate bars are easy and will have your lover thinking you sweated in the kitchen all day! Happy Valentine's Day, lovers!

INGREDIENTS

1 cup finely chopped cacao butter
3-5 Tbsp maple syrup or agave nectar
½ cup cacao powder
1 tsp vanilla extract
pinch sea salt (optional, plus more to taste)
cacao nibs (optional, for topping)

HOW TO MAKE A DOUBLE BOILER, IF YOU DO NOT HAVE ONE

1. Add 2 inches of water to a large saucepan and bring to a boil over medium heat.

2. Set a glass or ceramic mixing bowl on top (big enough so it does not fall in), making sure it's not touching the water.

DIRECTIONS

1. Add finely chopped cocoa butter to the mixing bowl and let melt for 2-3 minutes.

2. Once melted, add the maple syrup or agave nectar and use a whisk or wooden spoon to mix until fluid and thoroughly combined.

3. Remove bowl and set on a flat surface. Also, turn off stove-top heat and set saucepan aside.

4. Add cacao or cocoa powder, vanilla (optional), and sea salt (optional), and whisk to combine until there are no clumps.

5. Taste and adjust flavor as needed. I used about 3 tablespoons agave total and a pinch more salt (using minimum agave and more salt, overall)

but it's completely up to how sweet you prefer your chocolate.

6. Pour in evenly across chocolate bar molds or in a parchment-lined sheet tray, to cover all areas of the mold or sheet tray. If there are bubbles just lightly tap the mold or sheet tray on the counter a few times.

7. Lay flat in the refrigerator for about 2 hours to set. When set, flip over mold or sheet tray on clean surface and lightly tap out chocolate slabs onto counter. You can cut the chocolate into bars (unless you already used molds), or simply break off and enjoy!

Copyright © 2019 by Andrea Abedi.

Juliet Marillier is a multi Aurealis, Tin Duck, and Sir Julius Vogel Award winner and recipient of the Le Prix Imaginales for her historical fantasy fiction. Her novels are published simultaneously by major publishers in United States and Australia and are translated into other languages all around the world. Known for combining folkloric fantasy with historical fiction, her novels are often filled with sensitive depictions of the transformative journey a person can go through, metaphorically and physically, to protect their family and future partner—even characters who once thought themselves too broken or incapable of love. Born in New Zealand, Juliet now resides in Western Australia with a delightful menagerie of elderly dogs.

HEART'S KISS INTERVIEWS JULIET MARILLIER

by Lezli Robyn

Lezli Robyn: I had the pleasure of meeting Juliet Marillier online, on the nineteenth of June, 2009, but I had already been immersing myself in her fiction for a decade, since my twin sister and I discovered her first book, *Daughter of the Forest*, in our favorite Aussie bookstore on the Melbourne Peninsula. We were mesmerized by the folktales woven into her historical novels, and by the warmth of her characters. Her romances swept us away.

Last year, I finally had the pleasure of catching up with Juliet in person for a hot cuppa and conversation, and she was even more wonderful than her books. When it came time for me to do my first interview for *Heart's Kiss*, I could not think of a better romance author, now a dear friend, to ask.

Juliet, let us start with the obligatory first question. You graduated from the University of Otago with a BA in languages and a bachelor of music, teaching in both high school and university positions, as well as conducting choral groups. What prompted you to make the leap to becoming full-time author?

Juliet Marillier: It wasn't so much a leap as a very gradual transition. I did a lot of creative writing as a child and young adult, then veered toward my other love, music, working in that field for quite a few years. Later on I worked as a public servant. During that time I also raised my four children. I didn't start writing fiction seriously until I'd made a lot of life errors and grown wiser as a result. I wrote *Daughter of the Forest* while I was a solo parent working full time. It was written at least partly as therapy after some challenging times in my personal life. At that point I had no real thoughts of becoming a published author, let alone a full time one. But I did find that at last (in my forties) I had the space for my imagination to work, and I squeezed in the time to write because I passionately wanted to tell that particular story. My manuscript was picked up from the slush pile at Pan Macmillan and the rest, as they say, is history. I made the transition out of the public service job over four years, going gradually more and more part time as it became apparent I could actually make a living as a novelist.

LR: Your books are often filled with rich folkloric and historical content, yet you have also created settings that have a distinctive feel only experienced when reading your novels. How do you decide how much factual research you are going to include in your books versus fantasy extrapolation and innovation to balance out the blending of the two into a believable world and narrative?

JM: Great question! I like to base my settings on real world history and geography, but with that underlay of folklore and the uncanny, which I try to base on what the people of that time and place might have believed. I hope that helps make the magical elements believable to the reader too. Some of my novels have in-depth historical research behind them and it shows. For instance, *Wolfskin*, the first book of my Viking duology, required a huge amount of reading and some travel to back it up. If you visit Mainland in Orkney you can walk around most of the locations in that story! My Bridei Chronicles, set in the kingdom of the Picts, also has solid research behind it, but because we know less about Pictish history and culture there was more scope for informed guesswork and occasionally pure imagination. The "gray areas" of history, those about which there is some doubt, are fertile ground for the historical novelist. In my earlier novels, the Sevenwaters series in particular, I didn't yet realize

how important accurate history can be in a fantasy novel, and if I had my time again there are quite a few things I would change.

LR: You often write heroines and heroes in your books who can be considered flawed in some emotional or physical capacity. Whether they are warriors afraid of the dark and small places, or women with a powerful legacy who were born with a genetic deformity, I admire how you do not simply erase that flaw—make them perfect—by the end of the book, but make them face it, and learn to find strength and love *around* the imperfections in their life. I was afraid of the dark as a child, and closed spaces, and so I could identify so clearly with your character, Bran, from *Son of the Shadows*, in big part because he was *still* dealing with the ghost of those fears in adulthood. How much conscious effort is placed in writing lead characters who are dealing with the emotional and physical difficulties we deal with in real life, instead of creating a character of pure escapism for the reader?

JM: A lot of conscious effort. I try to get the psychology right, not only through research but by thinking myself into the mind of the character. I'm definitely choosing to feature more damaged characters now. It may be because a wider range of readers can see aspects of themselves there, or because that damage makes the character far more interesting to write about (and to read about) or because it's a better reflection of real life, which is low on perfect heroes. In the Blackthorn & Grim series the two protagonists are both suffering from PTSD and it governs their reactions and choices in some surprising ways. I had been reading a lot about military PTSD, especially in soldiers deployed to Iraq and Afghanistan, and how difficult it is for those soldiers to adjust after the return home. I did want to write about that issue, and I seem to have succeeded as I have had some magnificent feedback not only from readers who have PTSD but also from carers. I loved exploring the ways in which the various characters in the series find they are able to help one another. Another thing I loved doing was creating antagonists/villains who were three-dimensional. One of the wisest pieces of advice on characterization is that every character is the hero of his or her own journey.

LR: You had your first short story collection, *Prickle Moon*, published by Ticonderoga Press in 2013. Since this is a magazine specializing in short fiction, can you tell us how a writer so used to excelling in novel length publications found the process of writing romance in short form?

JM: Challenging, but rewarding. The short story doesn't allow much space for character building, plot development, internal monologues, etc. The writer needs to imply things subtly, not spell them out, and the reader needs to be able to make leaps of logic and imagination. Short stories require a lot of paring down and polishing, choosing the perfect word, shaping the perfect sentence and paragraph, and, of course, packing maximum emotional punch. I think short stories provide good practice for writing better—I hope I waste fewer words now when I'm writing long fiction!

LR: If you could pick only one of your books to be seen as your legacy in the world, what would it be, and why?

JM: Oh, that is so hard, especially as so many of them work as part of a series. If I really have to, I will pick *Son of the Shadows*. Although Grim is my favorite male protagonist, I am very fond of the "painted man," Bran, and I love his band of tattooed warriors so much I brought them back in a later series! That's possibly my most romantic novel.

LR: When you first started out, were you always intending to do a romance? Or was your original focus to do a folkloric fantasy and the sweeping romances that developed just grew out of instinct for what was right in the story? The relationships you have created between your lead characters are breathtaking and so full of heart and sensitivity.

JM: Thank you, what a lovely thing to say! I didn't set out to write a romance, but to develop and extend a favorite fairy tale into a deeper and more complex story. Of course, that fairy tale, *The Six Swans*, is quite a romantic one. But I think my novels owe something to my reading preferences. I love a good love story and some of my favorite novels have quirky or surprising romances in them. As a teenager I loved *Jane Eyre*. That was no doubt a clue to the direction I would later take as a writer.

LR: If you had to create a new couple out of a hero and heroine that were main characters from separate books of yours, who would you put together and why? Who do you think could be a good fit, even though they were originally created for different people?

JM: Another great question. How about Creidhe from *Foxmask* paired with Anluan, the "beast" character from *Heart's Blood*? She is a very practical young woman who just happens to be able to create magical embroidery, and she would take charge of the damaged Anluan's life quite well, I think! And she wouldn't care what he looked like. Or Neryn from the Shadowfell series with Darragh, the boy-next-door from *Child of the Prophecy*. He would be kind to her, as he was to the difficult Fainne. And they are both characters who are strong of heart.

LR: Is there any of your books, or series, you have written that was harder for you to complete, or took longer, for emotional reasons or due to the complexity of the content, and why?

JM: Probably the novel that will be next to come out, *The Harp of Kings*. My agent presented me with some challenges when we discussed the initial proposal—to make it shorter than my previous novels, faster paced, and a few other things. It was probably good for me to be jolted out of my comfort zone, but it did make the novel harder to write. I was extremely relieved when it found a publisher, and even more pleased when they gave the finished manuscript the tick of approval.

LR: Which book (or series) was it when you realized you've "made it" as an author? Was it a specific publication, or an award or recognition you achieved?

JM: I'm not sure I ever thought I'd "made it" but I realized I had a career when I started to earn enough from writing to support myself and my teenage son so I could give up the day job. That would have been when my third series, the Bridei Chronicles, was picked up by publishers in Australia, the UK and the USA. I never get complacent, though. An author is only as good as the next contract.

LR: If you had any advice for young authors, wishing to be the next Juliet Marillier, what would you tell them?

JM: Don't be the next me, be yourself! Write the story that's bursting to come out, not the story you think will suit the market. Recognize that you won't suddenly get rich and famous, and work hard at your craft. Read as widely as you can, well outside the genre you write in. Write because you love to write.

LR: Who are the authors that inspired you? Who helped you find your own voice as an author, and why?

JM: By far the strongest inspiration comes from traditional stories: myths, legends, folklore and fairy tales. I devoured those as a child and I still read them, as well as contemporary versions of fairy tales and scholarly books about them. When young I had an obsessive love for Tolkien. Growing up and developing my writing skills, I loved authors who combined great storytelling with elegant, clear prose: Daphne du Maurier, Dorothy L. Sayers, Mary Stewart. Scottish writer of historical fiction, the late Dorothy Dunnett, has long been a favorite for her rich historical tapestries, complex plots and unforgettable flawed characters. My own voice as a writer may owe a little to all those influences, and to some more recent writers too, but I know the main inspiration is those traditional stories. Then there's my background as a musician, which I think shows in the rhythms of my writing.

LR: What are the books you are currently reading now? How do they help you as an author, learning the craft? How do they help you escape from your own fiction?

JM: I've just finished an excellent fantasy, *Spinning Silver* by Naomi Novik. It's just as brilliantly written as her earlier fairy tale novel *Uprooted*, utterly absorbing and many-layered. A tale based around Slavic folklore and strong female characters. But mostly I've been reading detective stories and mysteries, which are my go-to reading when I'm writing a novel. They do help me escape, but they're also useful for learning about fast pacing and suspense. I love the Shetland series by Ann Cleeves, and I've

also been re-reading Kerry Greenwood's Phryne Fisher series, set in Melbourne in the 1920s.

LR: What is next for you? Are there new publications on the horizon we should know about?

JM: I have a novel called *Beautiful* coming out as an audio book from Audible. That is in production now and will be available, I hope, in the first half of 2019. It's based on the fairy tale *East of the Sun and West of the Moon*, and is told from an unusual point of view. *Beautiful* is for adult and young adult readers. Oh, and it is romantic, in a quirky way. In October 2019, the first novel in my new Warrior Bards series comes out from Penguin Random House US and Pan Macmillan Australia, and also in audio book from Recorded Books. It's called *The Harp of Kings* and features a training establishment for warriors and spies. The main narrator, Liobhan, is an accomplished musician and also a startlingly good fighter—a real departure from my previous female leads! I've had a sneak peek at the cover and it captures her intensity beautifully.

LR: How would you want to be remembered?

JM: As a writer whose work helped readers feel stronger, happier and more at peace with themselves. As a writer whose work helped inspire other people's creative efforts. I would also like to be remembered as the "brave, good and wise" person my characters strive to become. I still have some work to do before I get there!

Juliet's website: http://www.julietmarillier.com/
Facebook Fan Page: https:// www.facebook.com/ juliet.marillier/

CLOSING EDITORIAL
by Lezli Robyn

We hope you loved this issue as much as we did and are enjoying chocolates in the shape of hearts and sweet somethings with your significant other this upcoming Valentine's Day.

Tina Smith jokes in her editorial about me staging a coup from down under to overrun the magazine with Aussies (I'm staying with my family in Australia for a few months!) but in reality she had to pick up the reins for most of this issue while I dealt with the preparation and follow through of surgery—so I couldn't be more thankful and more proud to have such an amazing co-editor. It meant I never had to worry about the magazine being in good hands. It also meant I *did* add some more Aussie flavor into my content this issue, so she didn't miss me too much!

Over the next few issues we're bringing back some of our fan favorites. Harlequin author, Anna J. Stewart, returns to our pages with an exciting new novella set in the same paranormal universe as her Wardens series we published in issues 7, 8, and 9. Susan Donovan will be writing us another novella, this time exploring the happily-ever-after of Officer Partridge's sister, who first appeared in the Christmas novella she wrote for issue 12. We also have the exciting conclusion to L. Penelope's "Before I Break" in the upcoming issue and are thrilled to announce we'll be interviewing Christine Feehan in the coming months! So check back with us again when the next issue drops—or better yet, support us by buying a yearly subscription! We want to keep bringing you amazing content in this unique format for years to come, but we can't do it without your help. Thank you, dear readers, and happy loving.

www.HeartsKiss.com

Back Issues

Digital Subscriptions

Paper Subscriptions

...and more